EVERYBODY DESERVES A DISASTER

Melissa Walsh

MELBOURNE, AUSTRALIA

Melisa Walsh c/- Intertype
Unit 45, 125 Highbury Road
BURWOOD VIC 3125
www.intertype.com.au

Ordering Information:
Quantity sales. Special discounts are available on quantity purchases by corporations, associations, and others. For details, contact the "Special Sales Department" at the address above.

Everybody Deserves a Disaster / Melissa Walsh —1st ed.
ISBN 978-0-6487977-2-2

Contents

For my father who is my rock and the wisest man I have ever known, my mother who follows to the beat of her own drum, my children who are my greatest achievement, my sisters with whom I share a sacred bond, and my fiancé who has renewed my faith in relationships.

Thank you for your unconditional love.

"When disaster looms, all you have left is style."

David Carr

ACKNOWLEDGEMENT

To my father, my rock and my mentor. You taught me how to enjoy every moment, the good and the bad, to never give in and to handle challenges with grace and style. Without your guidance and faith in me, I could never have finished this book so this one's for you.

INTRODUCTION

The late writer, Nora Ephron, thought wit was a more powerful weapon than spite but I am not going to try to be funny in this book; telling you the truth is much more hilarious. When you find out what went on you may not believe me, but it all happened. After all, truth is stranger than fiction. What is probably the most bizarre when I think about it is how I could have made such bad choices. I made stinkers, whoppers and stupid decisions. Think of the worst-case scenario and then you are on the right track.

By far the most 'interesting' decision I made is where this story begins with husband number two (three years before Married at First Sight). He was a real catch, cheating on me, leaving the marriage, taking my money and even cutting off our power and phone. The guy was a natural born liar. He looked me straight in the eye and said he had never been unfaithful for years. Trust me, this much I knew. Even so, I am not going to share all of what happened. And while I would love to see him suffer, I don't think anyone would believe the enormity of what he did, so I will keep it to the relevant events, with a mixture of poetic license thrown in.

When I try to pick away at the carcass of that marriage and think about how it all got to the point of nasty, slimy, hitting the bottom of the barrel toxicity, I want to say it was all his fault. It's kind of easier when one person has been so low and debased that it makes the other partner look good. I would never try to pretend to fall into the role of angelic wife, where butter wouldn't melt in my mouth, because the truth is, in a way, I was partially to blame for the nightmare that ensued.

I know this because seventeen years earlier I broke up with my first husband, mainly because he was never home. He was starting a successful business and working all the time, so I left him. I thought that was as bad as it could get. Boy was I wrong! I also thought the grass was greener. Wrong again! Turns out, it's just different!

On my 50th birthday, my father said to me "It's this simple love. You can choose to have 50 years of experience or live the same life 50 times."

Dad always knew the right things to say. I knew what he meant but how to stop repeating the pattern?

The crazy thing is I am not a stupid woman. I am proud to say I now have two university degrees, a career as a journalist, one of the few who has lasted in print media for this long, and a healthy philosophical outlook on life thanks to my father, and lots of self-help books.

How did I let this happen?

When did it get to the point that I would lose everything?

And how would I ever pick myself up from this?

I have been very careful not to make my retelling of the past fall into a self-indulgent man bashing fest, which I have to say is very tempting. It's not that I hate men. I just hate the last man I married, but I will try to keep the melodrama to a minimum.

Life has certainly turned out different than what I had expected. I have loved and lost, have conquered fears and created new ones. I have seen people born and people die. I have made friends and lost some. I have had my fifteen minutes of 'fame' and now experienced firsthand what goes on behind the scenes of reality television, and the adventure continues.

At the end of the day, I know now that I had to lose everything in my life to find out who I truly was. I know I had to push the boundaries and jump headfirst out of my comfort zone to really live.

And I know that all the crazy things that happened were for my own good. And this is my story.

CHAPTER 1

LOSING THE HUSBAND

I learned my second husband was leaving at a barbecue. Not the ideal way to find out I admit, but then nothing was ideal in the relationship as I later discovered when his secret life was revealed. We were across the road at the neighbour's house celebrating her 55th birthday when he stood up and made the announcement. No if's, no buts and no eye contact with me at all. He did manage to muster a tear. After all the poor guy was devastated, he wouldn't be seeing the neighbours again and think of the time it would take to find someone else to drink with. Three years of marriage was apparently easy to say goodbye to but finding new drinking buddies, now that was a disaster.

There's nothing like a shock confession to change the whole mood of a gathering and suddenly we all knew that Kelly's birthday was no longer about her. He had a knack of making every occasion about him and he had managed to do it again. The night would no longer be known as a birthday celebration but "the day the neighbour told us he was leaving." It would be spoken about for years to come, a suburban legend that would possibly be altered and sensationalised over time. Suddenly the half-eaten chop and potato salad on my plate was unappealing and I reached for more wine.

As my Dad would say, I've had my fair share of misfires with men, but this one took me by surprise. Dad says my problem is I make decisions too quickly. He says the golden rule is this: "When it is a decision that won't have any long-term effects, make it as quickly as you like Missy. But when the decision will have an impact on your life, take as much time as you need to think about it." When was I going to learn?

I knew Dad was right but made the hasty decision anyhow and discovered that marrying someone 16 years younger with no real common interests is a disaster. Who would have thought? Anyhow, I had believed I was the exception to the rule and so we did get married after a couple of years. We had a beautiful wedding at a winery in the south, a little place we stumbled across on an afternoon drive one Sunday. The owners were just in the process of renovating and showed us around the property where the lake was being built at the front entrance, and a courtyard that captured the afternoon sun reminded me of Tuscany surrounded by vines and olive trees.

I was only 19 the first time I got married, scared and numb on the day, and wasn't actively involved in the planning. We had a baby boy and so my parents organised the whole thing. This time I knew what I wanted (not in a husband obviously, but definitely in the day). And it was everything I had dreamed of. The weather had been unseasonably stormy for February but when I woke up on the wedding day to see the sun was shining, I thought it was a good omen. Bruno, the ex-husband in question, had been watching the forecast obsessively on the BOM app he had downloaded on his phone as the event was outside and we didn't have a back-up plan, so we were off to a good start. My dress was divine, and I still have it in a big white box under my bed. Even though it was my second marriage, I insisted on wearing a long, white lace gown, and I felt like a princess.

My two oldest daughters, Antoinette and Vicky were bridesmaids, while my youngest Lizzy was the flower girl. Daniel, my son was one of the groomsmen, and had flown over from Kalgoorlie, where he was living, for the wedding. At 26, he had relocated to the west in the last four years and adored his life over there with his partner, Jen. Antoinette and Vicky wore beautiful floral gowns that Vicky had found in her online shopping ventures at Forever New. At 18, she had always been the stylist of the family and would often come in when I was going to a special occasion and before I knew it, she had chosen my outfit for me. She is the creative soul in the family, always painting and drawing, and keeps a keen eye on fashion. I still have her paintings displayed around my house.

There is only two years age gap between the two girls. They look alike with their fine Irish features and naturally brunette locks (which Vicky changes on a regular basis) and they have a wonderful bond, but completely different personalities. Antoinette, at 20, was studying law, and has always been driven; achieving everything she sets her mind to. Straight after VCE she took herself off to live in Ireland for a year, then came back to get stuck into her Bachelor of Law. My youngest, Lizzy, was the flower girl and, at just 9 years of age, loved getting dressed up in her white dress like me, and especially having her makeup done by the professional makeup artist that came to our home. She was a little put out that she couldn't have false eyelashes like her big sisters but got over it when we let her have chocolates before breakfast.

I was genuinely happy on the day, but I have always had this joke that "it's all downhill after the dress". Ironic how that amusing one-liner turned out to be a prophecy. Everyone at the wedding had a ball and my Dad, in his usual element, delivered the speech of the day. People still talk about that speech even now, but I was used to my Dad pulling out the big guns for special occasions. One particular part is etched in my heart: "Bruno, we are not alike at all. You are a great architect, you are a fabulous musician, you have a knack for technology. But there's one thing we have in common and that's we both love Melissa."

It was true. My Dad and he were nothing alike although I tried to pretend they were. My father is a small framed man, about five foot six but he has always told people he was taller. He has an air of dignity that comes with age and a wisdom from a long and adventurous life. Although the years show on his face, there is still a sparkle in his blue eyes. He loves his cravats and double-breasted suits and has always had a moustache which is now completely grey.

Bruno towers over both of us. (I got my height from my Dad). Standing about six foot two, he is a whole foot and two inches taller than me. He is a solid man, bordering on overweight at times. But he can get away with it because of his height. I liked that he was so tall. It made me feel safe. He could pick me up with one hand and often did when we were playing in the pool. You wouldn't call him a handsome man. He has very thinning hair and a weak loose chin that wiggled when he spoke, but he did look good to me when he got dressed up. There was always something in his eyes, however. They were so brown they were almost black. When we had arguments, I would look at those black eyes and think he might be evil.

We bought a house in Somerville not long after the wedding (the same house he left three years later). It was a four-bedroom red brick veneer with two big living areas and an in-ground pool that my youngest daughters were ecstatic about. It was their consolation prize like the million-dollar beachfront property we had all rented together when we first moved out. If they had to live with a stepfather, it may as well be somewhere nice.

The Somerville house was not my first choice, but Bruno loved it as soon as he saw the huge shed at the back that he would make into a man cave. The day we moved in that damn shed was carpeted and set up with the bar and couches before one item of furniture was unpacked in the house. I laughed at the absurdity of rolling out carpet strips for the cave and stocking the bar with footy and Ned Kelly paraphernalia while our furniture sat in plastic containers inside.

I always laughed when I was nervous and was trying to be the good little wife but deep down, I felt a sense of doom. It wasn't just that he was putting his own needs before the family. I had gotten used to that now and figured it was just a quirk of his personality that I had to live with. It was more sinister than that. I knew this would be his drinking place. He had always been a big drinker since the first day we met (at a bar of course) and I could tell that this was going to be a drinking room the moment he laid his eyes on the big stone bar that had been left as a fixture by the previous owners. Even on our first date, he met me at the door with a scotch in his hand and we got a taxi to the restaurant. It should have been a sign, but I didn't pay attention to my instincts back then and pushed anything I noticed deep down inside me and put on a smile. It's amazing what a desperate woman will dismiss but professionals like my psychologist have assured me that most narcissists (and he was a diagnosed narcissist) have a way of smooth talking. Even my Dad approved when he met him.

"You've won the lottery" he said to me in the early days, when I told him about this man who was an architect and now works in IT. And when we all moved into the beach house in Safety Beach, Dad called it "Hollywood" when he saw the view that stretched across the bay from Mt Martha to Sorrento.

I learnt he was either narcissistic or a borderline through the intense research one does faced with a situation they are desperately trying to understand. Within a few months of being married I would spend hours googling "what does it mean when your husband is wonderful at first and then dismisses you as unimportant, is unattached and unavailable?"

And in big blue letters there it was NARCISSIST. I'm sure this is a term that is bandied about these days, the psychological flavour of the month so to speak. But I could see real correlations between his behaviour and the signs and symptoms. He ticked nine of the ten boxes in every online test.

So, it's not surprising that it continued to go downhill when we moved into the Somerville home. What did surprise me was how quickly it fell apart, and my gradual inability to ignore the situation anymore.

The first night in our new home Bruno discovered the neighbours also loved a drink. The moving van had brought all our furniture from the Safety Beach house and the new furniture from Super Amart we had bought together (with the money from the sale of my own house, mind you) were stacked up in the lounge room. Boxes were spread all over the house, but the beds were all made up, so we had a place to sleep. He grabbed a six pack of beer and headed next door to Shelly and Paul's house. I liked Shelly as soon as I met her over the fence when I came to get the keys at settlement. She is a local policewoman, tall with dark hair and a solid build. The type of woman you wouldn't want to mess with. I could imagine her as the perfect cop, with just the right amount of toughness but a huge heart. Paul is a truck driver, a real aussie down to earth bloke with a no bullshit attitude, but he was kind. They had only just moved in together even though they were both middle aged. It was their second marriage and they were old friends from school who reunited years later over Facebook when Paul's marriage had broken down.

Very quickly they became his new best friends, and he partied with them till the early hours. When he finally got home, and threw up all over our bedroom, I knew I had made a mistake. What the hell was I doing? I had sold my own little home in Tyabb for this. I hated myself and hated my life. After he stumbled into the roman blinds and then made it to the bed, he lapsed into a snoring coma, so I left him there and went to sleep in my daughter's room.

Funny the thoughts that go through your mind when life hands you these moments. I lay next to my sleeping 10-year-old thinking of Nora Ephron's book 'Heartburn'. Her first reaction when she discovered her husband was cheating on her was "When can I date?" and it still makes me laugh to this day. I couldn't see myself ever out there again if this thing fell apart. Okay the marriage wasn't necessarily over but, hell, it wasn't looking too flash right now. I thought about how people cope with dramas in their life and wondered if I keep inviting this type of misfortune. I wondered how long it took for Nora to see the funny side of her situation and if I would ever see the funny side to this.

About now you must be thinking what is wrong with this woman. Why did she stay in that? And trust me, it's something I ask myself years later, but I have also learnt that it is my big mistakes that have brought me to my new life now.

I was also determined that I would not be divorced twice. Come hell or high water, this goddamn marriage was going to work. I have also learnt that, as my sister reminds me, we are not in control of anything, and so three years later, I found myself sitting at a barbecue when my husband stood up and announced that this was the last time they would see him, as he was moving out tomorrow.

CHAPTER 2

I SHOULDA KNOWN BETTER

I nearly fell off my chair. Not only was he telling the neighbours he was leaving before he told me, but he was more upset to be saying goodbye to them. The tears said it all.

Shelly looked at me and said, "That was the first you'd heard of it wasn't it?"

I shouldn't have been surprised when the announcement was made and yet he caught me off guard. He had a knack of doing that - just when you thought things couldn't get worse, he would bring it down to a whole new level. I sat there, looking at this weeping man who had just dropped a bombshell and it all seemed so surreal.

"What did he say?" I kept saying to Shelly. "That he is leaving tomorrow honey," she said in the kindest voice, as if saying it gently would lessen the impact. Bloody hell, I thought we were just coming to a barbecue!

If he was after a reaction, he certainly got one as all the neighbours were stunned, looking towards me for some explanation. He said he wanted to be alone and walked across the road to the house where we lived. He didn't want me there.

"What the hell was that about?" they all asked in unison.

"Welcome to my world" I thought but didn't say out loud.

I guess that's one of the good things about being with somebody who is constantly changing. You get accustomed to upheaval and, while not great, its somehow not as disconcerting. And boy did things change all the time? From quitting his job without notice or discussion (voice message on my mobile -"sweetie I have just quit my job, feel relieved, see you tonight"), to growing a beard (it didn't make you Ned Kelly by the way), buying a Harley (including leathers and beer gut) to reading the bible (passage discussion weekly) or obsessively researching conspiracy theories (apparently the world was going to end so garage gets stocked with water bottles, bags of rice and canned goods - NEVER HAPPENED!)

Yet, just as he said, he moved out the next day, filling his four-wheel drive with as much as he could take. "I'll come back later in the week to collect the rest of my stuff," he said to me as he was heading out the door, as if it was something we had agreed on.

I didn't think he would do it. I thought he would turn around and apologise and it would all be over. I kept thinking it even as the big grey monster of a car pulled out of the driveway. And then he was gone.

The relationship had always been tumultuous, and I often had anxious thoughts about my choice of husband. Even in the early days I was paranoid that he was playing around or, at the very least, not good enough as a partner. When we went to parties, he would often get so caught up with other people I would be forgotten. He didn't start off this way. In the beginning he was very charming, and I was a pushover.

He was a big tall man, larger than life, and everything he did reflected that. He spent money on lavish gifts. On our first Christmas together, he gave me a diamond bracelet and we had only been seeing each other for a month. He took me to lavish restaurants and spoilt me with exotic trips overseas. But something still didn't sit right with me. I felt like I was sleeping with the enemy and could never really let my guard down.

My good friend, Lisa, came to visit us when we first moved out together to the Safety Beach house. We were standing in the designer kitchen with its marble benchtops and view over the ocean and Lisa said, "you don't feel comfortable here do you?" Funny how sometimes your friends can mirror things you are too scared to say out loud, but I dismissed it as my usual case of anxiety and went back to denial any time I had the feeling.

This was not the life my father had dreamed for me despite the ostentatious property and new cars. I knew it deep down because my soul was disappearing, and I was losing my voice. I had become one of those women who don't speak their mind, and this was not the role model I wanted my children to see. But as the years went on, I got in deeper and deeper. We were joined in matrimony; we were joined financially, and I had this nagging feeling that I didn't want my children to see another marriage breakup. Strange how we justify our decisions and yet life has its own plans for us all anyhow. The truth is I knew all along this was not the right relationship for me. We always know the truth but have to wait until we are ready to say it out loud.

And so here I was once again, alone, packing up boxes and trying to find a place for Lizzy and me to live.

One thing I have discovered is that life is always full of contradictions. For every negative, there is a positive and my children were certainly enjoying some bright moments in their lives. Vicky by this stage had moved out with her partner and had given birth to a beautiful baby girl, who became a symbol of hope for me in my darkest days.

I was embarrassed that this had happened again, that my children were seeing me make such bad decisions with men. At the same time, my oldest son, Daniel, was coming down to Melbourne to get married. He and his fiancé Jen were living in Darwin, after relocating from Kalgoorlie where they had spent the past seven years building a life.

The idea of facing my first ex-husband and all the relatives at that wedding was overwhelming but I love my son and knew I wanted this time to be about him, not his mother's stupid mistakes.

Bruno, however, had a different plan. The weeks went by. He had cut off our power, phone and gas, but decided the day that Daniel and Jen arrived was the day he would come over to get the rest of his belongings. The kids and I had been out to a lovely lunch to arrive home to the police with Bruno and his mother outside the house. He had told them that I wouldn't let him in and called them to supervise. His mother Danya had always been a nightmare, and never liked me as I was so much older than her son. At family events she would introduce me as "this is his wife Melissa, she's 16 years older than him and has four children, can you believe that?" I hated spending time with her but still encouraged the relationship between them as they had been estranged for many years. Even when she decided to become a born again Christian and had the people from her church come around to exorcise the devil out of me, I still let her in the house. She had sent Bruno a five-page letter saying all the things she didn't like about me and he had asked me to humour her to get her off our case. Should have been a sign I know but, to my stupidity, I let them in that day, made them coffee and was the perfect hostess. Danya was not impressed.

So now here this woman was at my door again, delighting in the fact she had her son back. I already knew the part she had played in the decline when I logged into Bruno's Facebook one day to try and find answers as to why he disappeared. It was pretty easy to work out the password as it is the one he used on our home computer. There were messages between him and a young guy who he had hooked up with at a party the week he left (what the hell? I know. Crazy, right?). Ironically, these weren't the messages that disturbed me the most. It was the discussion with his mother that jumped off the page at me. I couldn't believe what I was reading. "I'm so glad you've finally woken up to her. I never trusted her from day one. She was always just after your money. Show up one day when you know she's at work and take the lot, that'll show the bitch."

I could go on, but you get the gist.

As Bruno stood in the kitchen dividing the cutlery and crockery, I could not stop crying. Every single plate he wrapped in newspaper cut me to the core. He was cold and detached and clearly trying to make a point. I didn't know if I wanted him back or to kill him. I think kill. He had shaved the beard, sold the Harley and was losing weight again. "Getting in shape for your next victim?" I thought to myself.

I was devastated that I had let it get this far, and that my children were there to witness the fallout.

I looked at my daughters and noticed how calm and together they were. When did they get so grown up? How could they be so self-possessed with a mother like me? These kids really had their heads screwed on right. Everybody said so. "What wonderful children you have Melissa. They are all so different but so driven. You must be so proud."

Of course, I was proud of my babies, but I couldn't help thinking it was more a result of nature than nurture especially in light of my recent disaster.

I didn't know how I would ever come back from this. I know that time heals and as my grandmother used to say "this too shall pass" but surely it was time to learn something. I had just turned 50 for God's sake and couldn't believe I was in a situation like this.

And then there was the issue of my sisters. I had always been the black sheep of the family, with a baby at 19, and now two failed marriages. They were the "good ones". The youngest, Leslie, is a psychologist who has been married to the same man for her life (unlike me), and she still owns her home (now I will be renting). The middle sister, Samantha runs her own business, and has avoided the pitfalls of relationships (definitely not like me). How could I face them again? This was supposed to be the relationship I settled down into; not the one that caused the most chaos.

It's not that I was the boy crazy one of the three of us. Both my little sisters had their fair share of young men 'sniffing around' as Dad would say, when we were growing up. Difference was they knew when to stop, and that was something that I had never figured out. I felt like one of those uneducated women on Jerry Springer who jump from one relationship to the next, losing their teeth and manners along the way, yelling and screaming with no sense of decorum or self-respect. Dear God, surely I wasn't the same as them. Sure, I had made some unfortunate choices with men, but I was a smart, employed and educated woman. Maybe that made it worse. Perhaps I should have known better.

There is something about me and the "10" birthday though. I broke up with my first husband when I turned 30, even though we had been together for 14 years and had three children. When I was 40, I broke up with Lizzy's Dad after a fleeting two-year relationship. My friend Lisa and I had this joke "We spend the first six months trying to get into a relationship and the next five years trying to get out."

It was true. I was addicted to being in love, but I had the feeling this time I might be cured. It made me feel better about myself that a smart woman like Lisa had done the same thing in her life too. She is a professor and runs a major company, but she had also been married twice to the wrong men, both ending in disaster. Like me, her second marriage was to someone younger. His name was Sebastian and he was very good looking but, as she soon found out, incredibly controlling, and it took her a long time to break free of the toxic relationship, and even longer to recover.

I was just like Lisa when Bruno and I finished, a mere shell of a person, spending days and weeks inside the house just sobbing, those snotty heartfelt tears that feel like they are coming out from the pit of your stomach. I didn't know it was possible to cry that much and had the attractive constant red nose and puffy eyes. One day, after he had come through and taken all his furniture, I collapsed on the floor of our bedroom where the bed once was and howled. The only thing left was the dust that had settled under the bed in a perfect rectangle on the charcoal carpet. The red wine splatters where Bruno had thrown up that night were still slightly visible on the cream blinds and, as I looked out to the lounge room there was nothing left but a pile of tangled cords where the stereo and television once stood. The neighbours Shelly and Paul had seen the moving van and came to see if I was okay, but I couldn't bring myself to get off the floor. They swept and cleaned and tried their best to untangle the cords but they were a mess like my life was and so we just threw them out.

CHAPTER 3

LOSING THE HOUSE

It's probably important to mention at this time that I was also broke. When Bruno and I got together I owned a little house in Tyabb where I had raised my children after my first divorce. I scrimped and saved to pay the mortgage on that house, at times living on minced meat and sausages and we all loved it there. I had even thought that one day I would be able to pass it down to the kids but that changed when he and I decided to buy a house together and we needed the money for a down payment.

Even though he earned a great income (300k a year – it still shocks me to say it) at a big architectural firm, he still didn't have any money to his name and plenty of credit card debt. He had cars, boats and a motorbike, and an amazing income but no actual money. I often thought it was strange that I could own a house on my meagre wage of $50,000 a year while raising four kids and he have nothing. So, we sold my house, paid off his debts and bought the new home together. I never really understood where the money all went but Bruno had insisted that he take care of the finances, as it was something his first wife would never let him do.

"She was so controlling Melissa. I love that you let me take charge and be myself. Thank you for having faith that I know what I am doing," he would say.

Fuck...... Now I know why she didn't let him control the finances. Sure, the bills were paid (most of the time) but there was never anything left over. After three years of marriage it mystified me that we had no money whatsoever and virtually no equity in the house.

It wasn't until six months after we broke up that the truth came out. I had known that he spent a lot of money on alcohol and had also developed a habit for smoking marijuana, but I had not known about the infidelity until sometime after the breakup. And then all of a sudden, the penny dropped.

Bruno broke the news to me that he had been sleeping with prostitutes when he was driving me to university one morning after I had lost my driver's license. After the marriage breakup I was a wreck, not eating enough and drinking way too much. Ironically the night I lost my license I had only had two drinks but still blew a massive .082 on the breathalyser. Bruno, by this stage, had found God (again) and was being remorseful, trying to make amends for everything that had happened. So, I was allowing him to drive me to uni as it was one of the only things I could still feel proud of.

I was doing my graduate degree in arts and writing a 40,000-word thesis so had to meet up with my supervisor every Wednesday as part of the prerequisite. I had no other way of getting there as it was all the way in Clayton and there is very little public transport from the peninsula, so Bruno was my only choice. I also figured he owed me so would put up with the 55-minute drive I had to endure with him.

Most mornings I followed my Dad's advice: "Never let the bastards know you're hurting". But not this day.

We had been driving along for about 15 minutes and, as he always did, Bruno was ogling me. He was desperate for us to get back together or, at the very least, me forgive him. And so, he watched me intensely all the time. His gaze made me feel like I couldn't breathe and so I pretty much always tried to diffuse the situation by making small talk.

"Gee the traffic's busy today. Thanks for the lift" or "I just saw a great movie last night I think you might like." That sort of thing.

Bruno of course, always tried to bring the conversation back to us. Well him actually. How he had been feeling. How sorry he was for everything. How he is really struggling at the moment. How he misses me and doesn't know if he can survive.

This particular morning, he didn't. The longer I was in the car the more intense the mood became until he turned to me and said "Sweety (I hated that he still thought he had the right to call me sweety) I have to tell you something. It will seem like bad news, but it is actually a gift."

What the fuck? Seriously?

Then "I don't think I should tell you today before you have to meet with your supervisor. I will wait till another time but all I can say is I have had an epiphany and I think in the long run it will be very freeing."

My heart was leaping into my throat. What more could he possibly tell me or do to me? I had no money, no house, and very little dignity because of him. And there was more? Apart from that you can't do that to a person. Say I've got something important to tell you then say I'll tell you later.

"That is bullshit. You have to tell me now. Otherwise my imagination is going to run wild."

He turned to me and said, "Are you sure you want to know now?" and I nodded "yes".

Then it happened. He said it – the thing I always dreaded: "You know all those times you asked me if I was being unfaithful when I went away on business trips and every time I said no. Well I have actually just remembered that I was, and I am so sorry. I just didn't want you to think you were going mad when you were actually spot on for all those years."

"I'm sorry. What? With whom?" I said, feeling all the blood rushing to my face. I thought I was going to faint.

"Well I have been having all of these memories lately of things that I must have blocked out of my mind but if it helps I have made a timeline of all the trips I took in the last five years, where they were and who I remember sleeping with. Most of the time it was in Thailand and Singapore and they were girls I picked up in bars." And then "I know this is really hard for you to digest but I am thinking of it like if someone gives you a gift that is wrapped in dog poo but inside it is a diamond."

What the hell? The tears were rolling down my face just like Muriel in Muriel's Wedding when she sits there uncontrollably crying at a restaurant when her girlfriends are teasing her. I could not stop, and I could not look at him. What do you say to that? How was I supposed to react? A gift? God he was full of shit.

Just to torture myself even more (and I don't know why we do this) I wanted details. Luckily for me he had made a spreadsheet of the infidelity.

"I want to know everything you remember. Did you have sex? Did you kiss? Did they stay the night? How could you do that and then come back to me? And when did this all start?"

He reluctantly told me the things he could remember. Being in a bar in Bangkok where the girls all line up and you choose which one you want, then pay a leaving fee to the bar owner to take the girls back to your hotel. Waking up in the morning feeling terrible that he had done it again. Having to face his co-worker Gregory who I had met and got on very well with. And then flying home to me knowing what he had done and determined never to do it again.

My questions kept coming. I hadn't tortured myself enough. "How could you come back to me after doing that? And what about all those times I said I had a bad feeling about you being unfaithful when you went away. Why did you not put me out of my misery and tell me then?"

I had no proof that Bruno had been cheating for all those years but every time he went away, I felt sick. I couldn't get it out of my head and finally had to go to a psychologist to help me deal with these insecurities.

She said I had nothing to worry about and gave me strategies to deal with the anxiety when he was on work trips. It hadn't helped but I had stopped asking him so much as the years went on as I was worried about pushing him away. I knew now that my instincts were spot on and I wasn't the crazy woman I thought I had been all those years. I would rather have been crazy.

For me this was the worst thing that could happen. I had always thought I would never cope with infidelity and it was the one thing I was the most terrified of.

Now here I was, trapped in his car, and the truth was staring me in the face.

Bruno thought telling me this newly discovered information would be the only way we could get back together.

"I wanted you to know the truth about me so we can have a chance in the future."

Of course, that was never going to happen. Yes, I had struggled with the marriage breakup. I had forced myself to let go of something that I had been clinging to for dear life. He had twisted the knife, hit me to the core of my soul and I was alone again.

I couldn't get out of the car quick enough when we arrived at the uni campus.

He raced around to give me a hug and apologise and make sure I was okay. And then I said something that I had no idea was in me.

I looked him in the eye and said "I am going to be fine. You may have been unfaithful, you may have taken all my money, and broken my heart but I will not allow you to ruin my day."

I walked away with my head held high and knew that he was feeling worse than I was. As I walked across the traffic lights towards Building J where my supervisor was waiting, I could feel his eyes on me and I knew in that moment, I would survive.

I was finally free. I was sad of course and, at times during my meeting I had to look down at my notebook as the tears kept welling up in my eyes, but I felt incredibly strong. He had given me a gift, but it wasn't the gift he had anticipated. I knew in my heart the truth I had suspected all along, that this man was not worthy of my affection.

When I told people later about what had happened, they sometimes said "Did that make you feel bad about yourself in a sexual way that your husband went to prostitutes?" But it never did. I had clarity and I hadn't had that feeling in a long time. I knew I had been a bloody good wife. We had a good sex life; I was kind and I gave myself to him in every way. There is nothing more I could have done to make that marriage work. I was sad but he was the one who lost everything.

My Dad says that "We are born alone, and we die alone, and we are the ones who have to sleep with ourselves every night." It is a philosophy I have taken to my heart and it helped me to understand the importance of being honourable and true to yourself. I suspected this would be something that Bruno would never know.

So, this was how our story would end. The months of wondering if we might get back together, the flowers and "I'm sorry" gifts, the tears shed for a marriage I grieved, the propensity to think about the good times and dismiss the bad, and the reluctance to finally let go were over. And I was on the earth alone again. No more questions, and no more doubts. I was not just letting go of a marriage. I was letting go of a lifetime of looking for a man to make me whole. I learnt to take each day at a time and found joy again in the simplest moments.

And life went on. Before long, Bruno had stopped calling, knowing that his efforts to reunite were in vain. In the end he couldn't understand why I couldn't forgive him, and it took all my strength to not give in to his tears and sad stories about suicidal thoughts and child abuse that he had also remembered about.

But I knew that I could not live his life anymore. It was time for me to be the main character in my story and not an extra. For the first time I knew it was good to be alone. I was slowly discovering every day just how strong I was.

CHAPTER 4

HERE WE GO AGAIN

I hate moving. I'm sure not many people love it, but I particularly dislike it, as I tend to gather possessions. I'm not one of those crazy hoarders who live amongst piles of papers, boxes and rubbish that you see on reality tv, but I do collect "stuff". It just seems to grow and before I know it, I have overflowing wardrobes, drawers and cupboards. Mum was a 'stuffer'. The surfaces in her home were free of junk but you didn't dare open a cupboard door for fear of things falling out at you, and I definitely take after her in this way. That's why packing up is such a pain.

Lizzy and I were moving into a lovely townhouse in Hastings. It was not an area I wanted to live in but have grown to love it. Hastings is on the western port side of the peninsula. Some might say the poor relation to Mornington. It has a small beach on the foreshore where the pier is, but it is more mud than sand. It is a pretty spot but has a bad reputation with some rough neighbourhoods like west park which, thank god, we were nowhere near. My children had all gone to school there at the local catholic primary school, so I knew it well. I just never thought I would live there. The fact was I had to find somewhere that was affordable and close to public transport, as I had no license for six months. Lizzy found the house on the internet and we both loved it when we walked in.

It is a two-storey place made of sandstone and one of only four on the block. It is right across the road from a reserve and from the top floor you can see across the park to western port bay. Two smoke chimneys from the BHP plant shoot out flames that light up the sky in the evening, and for some reason, they give me comfort every time I see them. Downstairs is a kitchen, lounge and dining room and a bedroom for Lizzy. Upstairs is my bedroom and another large living area so each of us has our own space which I know from experience is a priority when you have a teenage daughter. We were downsizing quite considerably; four bedrooms to two, a single garage instead of an eight-car shed, one small dining area and lounge, so it was time to cull.

Fortunately, one of the great things about breaking up is you feel unattached to things. I couldn't care less about possessions at this time. Apart from my clothes and shoes and photo albums of the children, everything else meant nothing. I went through that house in Somerville like a woman possessed, chucking photos of the two of us into black plastic bags but not before I had ripped them to shreds. There's something empowering about throwing things out and I needed all the power I could get.

Our big walk in robe was only half full now. The inevitable, all too familiar sign that the marriage was over. As I walked into the wardrobe I tried not to picture where Bruno's clothes and shoes had been, but the empty space was tempting me to back into my dark misery. I remembered arguing over the closet space when we moved into that house. I had a lot of clothes and I mean a lot. I had always been a shopper and it astounded me just how much stuff I had collected. He was organized and, like most men, only shopped when he needed something. We would go out twice a year to his favourite menswear store and he would quickly choose two pairs of jeans, a few shirts, and maybe a jacket. He was meticulous and never strayed from his list, so his side of the wardrobe was neat and organized. Blue shirts then white shirts, ties on the tie rack, and shoes meticulously lined up. Mine was always messy with clothes piled three to a coat hanger, and drawers that were so full they could hardly close. Things that didn't fit in the wardrobe, I put in garbage bags and suitcases and stored them in the top of the wardrobe. Sometimes I just threw them up there, hoping they would stick.

"I don't know why you need so much Melissa" he would say. "Why don't you throw some of these things out? You never wear half this stuff."

I knew he was right, but I found it hard to get rid of things. Occasionally the mood would strike, and I would take everything out of the wardrobe and pile it up on the bed or the floor to sort. Most of the time I put it all back again, convinced I would wear them one day. His rule that "if you haven't worn it in a year it needs to go" didn't apply to me. "A year? Get serious," I often said to him.

A half empty wardrobe in a suburban house can be a lonely place but I had no time for self-pity, so I pulled out the moving boxes and started packing, hoping I didn't find any of his things amongst my piles of clothing. I have to say I am a bit embarrassed about how many clothes I have. "There must be a hell of a lot of money in that wardrobe" I thought as I folded dresses, skirts, jeans, scarves and hats into the boxes. There was no order to my packing. "Just throw it in and get it done as quickly as possible" is my theory. Sometimes I would label the boxes in thick black texta with "Melissa's dresses and skirts" or "Melissa's hats, scarves and belts". By the end of it, I'm lucky if I even bothered writing "Clothes".

A mild scent of aftershave in the wardrobe where his shirts once hung brought me back to my darkness and I wondered what he was doing now. I was still in shock about what had happened and every now and again my thoughts drifted back to him. Dad always taught us the importance of being in control of your mind. "Pain is inevitable. Misery is a choice "he would say. I tried not to wallow, but the temptation was too strong and before I knew it was playing my go to sad song of the time Boz Scaggs' "We're all alone". A few tears later and I was back. "No time for this. Pull yourself together" I said out loud to myself as I stared, reprimanding myself in the mirror. It took a whole day to pack up that wardrobe but, seven boxes and several garbage bags later, it was done.

CHAPTER 5

NOT THE DOG

There was only one thing left to do now and that was finding a home for our golden Labrador, Major.

The house Lizzy and I were moving into had no room for a dog, and Bruno said he didn't want him.

I know Labradors have a reputation for being crazy, but Major was crazy on steroids. We had bought him as a pup from a breeder in Ballarat when we first moved into the Somerville house. Bruno and Lizzy were so excited to have a dog, and he was cute. We realised how nutty he was the day we got him home. He raced straight into the backyard on this wet and miserable day and got wedged between the shed and a retaining wall. You don't know hard until you've tried to retract a wet, muddy, slippery puppy out from a small cavity, but we got there eventually. That day set up the ritual for how Major would be. If he wasn't barking, he was jumping and, if he wasn't jumping, he was eating the outdoor furniture. One day I came home from work to a sea of foam outside the kitchen window and Major sitting on the cane couches which now had no cushions looking very proud. He might have been a pain, but I still loved him and giving him away before we moved was one of the hardest things I've had to do.

Shelly our neighbour, had told me about a place that adopts Labradors and, apparently, they had a good reputation. They would find Major a home. The morning the lady came to pick him up I decided to let him in to play on my bed. He loved jumping up on the bed and this 60 kg beast thought he was a lap dog. I wanted to spend some time with him so let him in to play before she got there. When the van pulled up in the driveway, I was inconsolable. I swear the woman from the dog adoption agency didn't know what she had struck as I stood in the kitchen signing the paperwork for her to take Major away with tears streaming down my face. I couldn't even speak to her I was crying that much.

"I will go and get him and put him in the car" she said to me. "It's better if you just stay here." The poor woman couldn't get away quick enough. I wondered how many other divorced women she had retrieved labradors from. Probably wasn't a good idea to try and confide in her about the breakup. In hindsight, she really didn't need to know the nightmare that had ensued over the past months.

I watched out the kitchen window as she took Major away and it amazed me the control she had over him. In three years, I could never get him to stop jumping all over me, let alone have him walk beside me calmly like this woman was doing. He climbed into the van with no fuss and seemed excited to be going on an adventure. It was almost like he was doing it on purpose to show me up. You know what I mean? Like when your kids are hideous at home and then angels for others, as if somehow, it's about you.

I think about that crazy dog sometimes now, wonder where he ended up, and hope they found a family to love him. I like to think that he's on a big farm in the country where he can run free and that he's happy.

Before I knew it, moving day was here. It had only taken a few months for the Somerville house to sell and I decided to move out before settlement as we had found our new place in Hastings, and I didn't want to lose it.

The moving van pulled into the driveway at 7am sharp, like a beacon telling the neighbours that the relationship was really over. Within a couple of hours, the three movers had packed my life into their truck and were ready to take off. Sounds silly, but I felt like everybody knew that I had made another mistake and moving was the proof.

I've never been one who likes leaving a house and, even though this house had nothing but bad memories, the wave of sadness came over me when I shut the front door for the final time. I looked around at the garden beds I had made, the front fence that we painted out on a scorching hot January day, and the broken blind in the lounge and hoped the next owners would be happier there. Walking down the driveway to the car, I tried not to notice if any of the neighbours were looking. I was embarrassed and ashamed and determined that this was not the woman I wanted to be. The new house would be another chance to start again. This time would be different.

I breathed a sigh of relief when we pulled up to the new townhouse. This would be our sanctuary.

It was perfect for Lizzy and me. My bedroom was upstairs with a beautiful living room that looked over the western port bay with a reserve in the foreground, and Lizzy's bedroom downstairs next to the lounge and kitchen. If I had learnt anything from having four children, it's that parents and teenagers need their space, and this set up was ideal.

I remember my grandmother used to tell me how therapeutic it was to get your hands into the garden, so I planted some geraniums and palms in the lovely private courtyard at the back. "Comfort in the mundane" my Dad calls it and it has served me well over the years. When things get overwhelming, just do something domestic, plant some flowers, clean the house; it's incredible how consoling it can be.

I had been lost for so long and wanted to find myself again, so I started playing music. I would light my incense and listen to a favourite song. I even went out and bought myself an old record player which I put upstairs. And as the months went on, I started to remember how good life can be. Sure, I had no money, no husband, and actually no license, but I was free.

I even stopped shopping which had been a big coping mechanism for me during the breakup. They don't call it retail therapy for nothing and the extra clothes and shoes in the wardrobe were a sign of just how bad things had been.

I spent a lot of time in silence during those days. I wanted to be still and truly present. I had spent years buying self-help books but never really understood what they were saying. I put positive mantras around my room on post its. "You are perfect as you are." "Today is a new beginning". "Be present." My shelves were stacked high with Louise Hay, the Dalai Lama, Deepak Chopra all with fabulous words of wisdom that I wasn't ready to hear until now. It was okay to be where I was. It was time to let go of the guilt and shame and accept that this had all happened for a reason.

It was also okay to not know exactly what that reason was at the time. I had faith that, if I kept being true to myself, time would take care of the rest.

Of course, it wasn't all roses. There were times when the tears would start but I wasn't crying about the marriage. I was crying out of relief and a deeper self-understanding.

I realised things about myself that I had never known. (I am sure my Dad knew which is why he always looked out for me but finally I understood too.)

I always have to do things the hard way and find out by experience what I want and don't want in life. Perhaps we are all like that. I realised I had very low expectations for my life and that meant I was willing to accept anything. I realised that we are all in charge of our own destiny and never to rely on someone or something for happiness. I realised that you can never feel so alone than when you are with the wrong person. And all of this I found in the silence.

CHAPTER 6

WHAT WOULD THE DUCHESS DO?

When you have no money, are renting a house in the only town you can afford, and work at a minimum wage job you love, what else is there to do but incur a larger HECS debt? Well it made sense to me, so I decided to enrol at Monash University to do my post graduate degree. Doesn't it sound great? It's like you have to be smart just by being accepted for it. It wasn't for career advancement or money (although both of those would be great). It was because I wanted to learn something and make myself proud again. Part of the fallout of broken relationships is a low sense of self-worth. My self-esteem was in the gutter, so it was time to find some pride again.

There's a certain osmosis that happens just by walking into the grounds of a university, like all these smart minds, thinking and discovering new things will rub off. My father tells this joke: "Where are you if you are the smartest person in the room?" Then he says: "You're in the wrong room." I got that. I'm kind of like a walking contradiction and have been the smartest person in the room as often as I've been the dumbest. I love learning and going to university and hanging out with inquiring minds, but I also can get pissy at a local pub, watch reality tv, and get hooked on trashy magazines like the best of them. It's okay if you're confused. Trust me - I confuse myself.

I had gone to uni the first time after my son Daniel was born. I was a 19-year-old mum and wife and wanted to learn. When my Dad found out about the pregnancy, he said to me "The thing that makes me the saddest is that now this is all you will do" That was like a gauntlet to me. "I'll show you Dad, this is not all I will do."

For me, university is more than academic learning. I loved being around people who were thinking differently. I loved that at uni I was not a mum, a daughter, or an employee. I was a student with an open mind and excitement for learning. I think I'm going there just to get a degree, but it always ends up being so much more.

I'm a bit of a believer in signs and I knew the moment I walked into my supervisor's office; I was meant to be here. Outside his door was a huge poster of a lovely elderly poet, Gwen Harwood, who I later found out had passed away. Gwen and I had become instant friends when I was going to university 30 years before. She was a writer in residence and edited and mentored me on my first book about teenage pregnancy.

I was overwhelmed to see her there. I hadn't thought about Gwen for many years and started to feel bad that we hadn't kept in touch. That was a lifetime ago during my first marriage, but Gwen was one of those women who inspired just by taking an interest. She introduced me to the concept of being independent, and the idea that I had what it took to be a writer. After all these years there she was, still looking over me.

When I walked into Professor Grant's room, it did not disappoint. It was exactly what a literary scholar's office should be according to my romantic notion of English academics. Disheveled paperwork strewn across his desk showed he was far too busy with important literary pursuits for domestic trivialities like cleaning. Floor to ceiling shelves overflowing with books, holding that precious cargo of words that promise to stay with you for years, filled with timeless wisdom. It was all so exciting and scary. "I am definitely not the smartest person in the room here, Dad."

Professor Grant stood up from behind his desk to greet me as I walked into the room. His presence was intimidating but I couldn't tell if that was his arrogant air or my own insecurity. I felt a bit like a fraud being there and wasn't sure if I was quite smart enough to do a degree like this. After all, it had all started one day sitting at work and bored, checking out what courses were on offer. Before I knew it, I had applied and was accepted. I worked out the course I wanted to do and had the relevant tertiary qualifications to apply. My HECS could be deferred and I could fit the on-campus days around my work schedule easily. Apart from all this, I loved the name of the course 'Post graduate degree in English Literature (Research)'. Even the title was brilliant.

My tendency to act first and think later had resulted in me standing in the presence of this wealth of academic knowledge where I couldn't admit I had absolutely no idea of what I was doing. I guess that's the point of learning. To push yourself outside your boundaries, right?

Don't you just love it when life surprises you? That's how university has been for me every time. I know I'm going to feel good about myself. I know that my children and Dad will be proud. I know that I will learn something new, but the surprise comes in those unexpected moments that have a profound effect.

This time was no different.

After the usual introductions, Professor Grant asked me to sit down. He had a thick mane of grey hair, verging on all white, a bushy, disheveled beard and a strong English accent which made him sound even more intelligent. I wondered if he had a girlfriend, wife or even boyfriend. Not because I was interested in him, but I was curious about whether someone so smart would get caught up in emotional dramas like I had in the past.

"Do you know what you would like to do your thesis on?" he asked me straight away, his words firing at me like bullets. I have never written a thesis and wasn't quite sure what was involved but he seemed approachable so I figured I should be upfront and honest.

"I have absolutely no idea," I uttered, hearing the words coming out of my mouth and wishing I had been more discreet about my ignorance at the very least.

"Oh" he said, as he stroked his beard with his chunky fingers. "I see."

I sat there stunned. I knew I didn't belong there but hoped that he would help me anyhow.

"Well what sort of thing do you like studying?" he asked, as if he could see right through my facade.

All I could think of was the subjects we had done in the past year, so I pulled out of my hat: "Orientalism and dysphoria in literature?"

"Crock of shit" he spat out. "No, you don't want to be doing that. I know it's the flavour of the month, but it has no depth. No, just no."

I was secretly delighted he had this attitude. I hadn't really enjoyed the past subjects, but it had been my only experience with academic work since the 1980s and I wanted to seem even slightly prepared. I also loved that he was so passionate about literature, like someone who's obsessed with politics or religion. It was just what I needed to be around.

"My specialty is in the writings of John Webster," he went on to say. "He is a counterpart of Shakespeare and a playwright from the Jacobean era. Very underestimated but brilliant in his day. There are elements in his plays that are very forward thinking. Would you like to check some out and let me know next week if any of these appeal?"

With that, he gave me a heap of books from the mysterious John Webster. His shelves were piled high with books from the 17th century, authors that I have never heard of but who had sage advice amongst their pages. I had never heard of John Webster but trusted the professor's opinion already. We made a date to catch up the same time next week and I walked out of the office with a pile of books under my arm and a spring in my step. There are times in life when you know you are in the right place and this was one of them. I was living again.

It turns out this John Webster was an amazing writer and I was hooked from the first play I read, "The Duchess of Malfi".

This was what I would write my thesis on- this strong and independent woman who lived in the most suffocating and barbaric patriarchal society and continued to stay strong and stoic in the face of corruption and misogyny. Who would've thought such inspirational women could come out of a 17th century play? Let alone been a real woman, not just a fictional character.

The more I read about the duchess, the more I wanted to be like her. I even developed a saying "What would the duchess do?" in times when I was struggling emotionally.

I remember one time when Bruno was trying to ingratiate himself back into my life, I found myself being tempted to hear him out. I had always wanted to see the best in him and yet the facts were right in front of me. HE WAS NOT GOOD ENOUGH. Simple.

One particular night, after hours on the phone to him sobbing and sending me the saddest photos of himself dressed in a jester costume to try and find some inner happiness, I asked myself 'what would the duchess do?' It was so easy after that. She would be courteous, but not manipulated. She would graciously end the conversation with poise and style, and she would remain determined to not take on his sadness. She would look after herself.

In hindsight, it was something my Dad had always told me. "You have to be selfish, Missy," he would say. "You have to be arrogant and selfish. They are very misunderstood words. To be arrogant is to believe in yourself. It is to know your worth. To be selfish, is simply to put yourself first. That doesn't mean you don't feel compassion towards others, but their plight is not put before yours."

I finally was beginning to understand what my Dad had said all those years and what this beautiful and mistreated duchess had demonstrated. Love yourself enough to put yourself and your needs first. And, with a little practice, that is something I began to do.

Before I knew it, I was writing a 40,000-word thesis. I was reading literature reviews, learning to write in an academic way which is very different to feature writing. And I was learning from my new friends, Professor Grant and The Duchess how to be a better person.

The day I finished that thesis, I walked into the university with my head held high. It was only eight months, but I was a very different woman from the person who started there, scared and feeling unworthy. I didn't know what marks I would get but I knew, in my heart, I had done my best. When I gave my Dad a copy to read, he had to get his dictionary to look up some of the words, so I knew it must be fairly good as Dad is the most knowledgeable man I know (until Professor Grant of course.)

My thesis was called "The Monstrous Regiment of Women: Speech, Gender and Power in the plays of John Webster." And I still have copies of it in my house today. It constantly reminds me that it is possible to be strong and dignified in the face of disaster.

Like my Dad says, "The choice is always ours."

CHAPTER 7

THREE GIRLS IN NEW YORK

When my sisters and I were little we all shared the same room. We didn't need to. Mum and Dad had built a big house for us in Bulleen with four bedrooms, the master at the front and the three girls' bedrooms down the hall at the back. But we wanted to sleep together. My parents put all three beds into the biggest room, Leslie's the youngest sister, and we would giggle and chat till we fell asleep.

On special nights Dad would come in and tell us a story, usually it was a made-up story about Pegasus, and we would hold our breath in anticipation of what exciting adventure that big winged horse would take us on. We were always in the story. Pegasus would come to our room when the parents were asleep and tap on the window. Tap tap tap. Dad would do the actions by knocking his hand. Then one of us, usually Samantha the middle sister, would go to the window and Pegasus would tell her he wanted to take the three of us for a ride. We would get our brunch coats on and jump aboard the stallion. I would be up front as I was the oldest, Samantha in the middle and Leslie behind her and we would hang on for dear life. Pegasus would fly us up over our house and the neighbours' homes, we would fly over the school, and the shops and then far into the sky to a magical land.

The adventures were different every time and, to this day it still seems magical to me, as if my mind imagined it so vividly, I sometimes wonder if it really happened.

Occasionally, Dad would also sing us this song. I remember it distinctly because it terrified me, although I loved how he did the actions – holding his hand on his heart while he sang: "Your baby has gone down the plug hole, your baby has gone down the plug, the poor little mite was so thin and so slight, he could have been washed in a jug every night." He sang the last two words like a barber shop quartet and then "E–v-e-r-y n-i-g-h-t."

We used to roll around laughing but, at bath time, I always steered clear of the plug.

Dad has always encouraged us girls to keep our bond but, as we grew older, we grew apart. We went off on our own journey. I had my first baby at 19 and, ironically, went into labour in that exact same room where my little sisters and I used to sleep all those years ago. Samantha went off to London at just 21 and built a business there, continuing to travel all over Australia until she finally made a home in Sydney. And Leslie married her high school boyfriend and now has three children and has finally got her license as a psychologist after years and years of studying.

After many years making bad decisions with men, my sisters couldn't sit by and watch the chaos I was causing for my children particularly, so we started fighting. At birthday parties and family events, the girls would bring to my attention how it was affecting my children, but I was so far in denial I wouldn't listen. I look back now and know they were just a mirror for me but what I had done was too hard to bear so I fought against every personal attack. I look back now and know they were just scared for my children and me. I remember Samantha saying to me "These kids don't deserve this life Melissa. You have to grow up and start looking out for them. They are hurting and you don't even see it." But I wouldn't listen. Actually, I think I couldn't hear what she was saying because it wasn't my time yet.

Samantha, of course was right. In the early years, she had a very close relationship with my children. We would all go away on holidays together and spent most weekends hanging out together especially when Daniel was young. She was there when I found out I was pregnant the first time and supported me through making the decision to keep the baby. She even bought me a photo album to put all the pictures of my newborn baby once I had made the decision to keep him. In it was an inscription "To my new niece or nephew, this is something for you and your mummy to keep happy memories in." I still have it to this day.

I still spoke to my sisters and occasionally went to family events, but they became less frequent as the years went on. I went about living my life down on the peninsula, and the girls lived theirs. For many years we didn't see each other much and, as the time went on and my relationships broke down, I was too embarrassed to be around them.

I never would have guessed that I would get to know my sisters again in New York forty years later. My sister Samantha was celebrating her 50th birthday and had kept saying that she wanted to wake up in New York to celebrate. Leslie and I thought we should just throw her a party. How can three sisters just pack up and go to New York after all?

I had just moved into a new home after my second marriage breakup and was caring for my teenage daughter whose father was not exactly a responsible force in her life. Leslie still had a small child to look after as well as a reasonably new psychology practice she was just establishing in Pakenham. And Samantha had moved to Melbourne after a fallout with her business partner and was picking up and starting her life again.

It turns out life is what happens while you are making other plans because, within three weeks, we were all booking our flights to New York. How did this happen you may ask? Well, it was one of those times when everything just fell into place.

Two weeks before, I had a phone call from Leslie saying that she had decided to go. Her husband, George, could look after their youngest daughter and her work was her own practice so she would just rearrange clients.

"Do you think you could go, missy?" she said excitedly down the end of the line. "I know it's hard, but we have our accommodation paid for and so it's just air fares and spending money."

As a birthday gift to Samantha, our Dad was paying for the accommodation up to a few thousand.

"Wow I didn't know Dad was paying for that," I said. "Okay let me look at how much I have in savings and let you know."

The thought of going to New York with my sisters, or at all, is something I never considered could happen. I felt like I had made a mess of my life and that was so far out of reach. I had no money, apart from a little savings, had lost my home so had to rent, and my income was not particularly high from being a journalist at a local magazine.

I went and spoke to my Dad when I was trying to decide what to do. I desperately wanted to go. The more I thought about it, the more exciting the prospect became, but I made sure I kept myself composed because deep down I didn't really think it was possible.

Dad was living at his house in Mornington. He had moved to the peninsula to be closer to me as his country property was becoming too hard to handle and the last fires that surrounded him were actually scary instead of adrenalin boosting.

His little house was right near the ocean so he could still see his beloved horizons, and he walked the esplanade every day with his walker.

"Dad, I wanted to talk to you about New York. The girls are definitely going and I'm trying to decide if I should. I have made so many bad choices with money that I am scared to make another one," I said to him as he sat in his leather recliner with the matching footstool.

He looked at me and said: "Now I want you to listen to me. I couldn't think of anything better than you going to New York with your sisters. Its half the reason I am paying for the accommodation. If you can get together enough for the airfares and some extra spending money, you have to do it love."

And then he said something that stayed with me forever: "Everyone should see New York at least once in their lifetime."

My Dad always came out with gems like this. He was well travelled but not to boast or be someone different when he took trips. He always told me it was the only way to really grow, to learn about yourself, experience different cultures and then come back home appreciating where you live even more. Every time I go away to this day, I think of my Dad and what he taught me.

So, I did end up buying a ticket. I saved some spending money and I looked up things to do in New York every night. My sisters and I would be staying in Jersey City, right on the Hudson River. We had a fabulous apartment Samantha had found on Air Bnb and when we arrived, we went out to the balcony and could see the Statue of Liberty. I had to pinch myself.

I swear we were like three teenagers, full of excitement and adventure.

Our apartment was right on the Hudson, on the fourth floor of a huge building. It was open plan living with a pull-out couch that made a big bed, and a single separate bedroom.

Leslie and I were sharing the room with the queen-sized bed, and Samantha would have the lounge with the pull out. There was a balcony that looked over towards Manhattan and I never ever wanted to leave.

We unpacked our cases and decided to get a good rest as it had been a 22-hour flight and tomorrow was Samantha's birthday. She was actually going to wake up in New York just like she had planned.

Leslie and I were like those little kids in our old house, laughing till our stomachs hurt. I don't even know what about. It was so wonderful to feel such excitement and joy. I didn't know it existed and realised that life had really taken its toll on me that this happiness was so foreign. Not only was I going to see New York, I had already started to change my attitude and realised it was possible to be happy again.

The next morning, we woke bright and early, and went in with our birthday presents and a muffin with a candle in it, singing Happy Birthday to our sister. The ferry across to Manhattan was right outside our door so we decided to get dressed and have a day in New York doing whatever Samantha wanted to do. Everything was perfect. The Paulus Hook ferry arrived, and it had big letters across the front saying Liberty Ferry. We sat up on the top deck and looked out over the river as New York got closer and closer.

I had heard that New Yorkers are not very friendly. It is a small island with a lot of people who naturally keep to themselves, but our experience was quite the opposite. Every single person could not have been nicer. They helped us with maps, and where to find the best coffee (number one on Samantha's list), and I felt really at home there. That may have been because I am a huge fan of Sex and the City. Carrie Bradshaw has been my role model for years and I have found such comfort watching episode after episode of her relationship issues. So, I was kind of familiar with a lot of the places. We went to the New York City Library where, of course, she had her botched wedding. We went to Central Park and took a horse and carriage ride. We went to the empire state building where a saxophonist played 'happy birthday' to my sister, and then we jumped in a limousine to see a show on Broadway. It was honestly the best day I can ever remember. I was in New York, but what made it magic was seeing it with my sisters.

I looked at Leslie and Samantha and realised I had missed out on so many years with them. Samantha and I hadn't been close for a long time, and it was wonderful to have her back. Actually, I was just so thrilled that she wanted me there. As for Leslie, I hadn't realised how hilarious she is. We laughed all the time and, for the first time ever, we uncovered a very deep connection which I will always be grateful to New York for.

The next two weeks were heaven. Every day we got up, dressed and jumped on our ferry. Very soon, we felt like locals, wandering around town, checking out theatres, galleries and restaurants. We even got used to the sirens which are constant background noise. Of course, we did all the 'New York must do's' on our extensive list. I actually can't believe how much we saw but still had time to sit in a park and take it all in.

Leslie had a sore foot for the entire time but managed to deal with the pain with the help of tequila. She had never been a drinker (I had made up for both my sisters in that department.) Samantha is Muslim so she didn't drink alcohol either. Dad had always instilled in me the importance of marking an occasion and, in typical Irish catholic form, this often-included good food and wine. We had Bollinger on Christmas morning, and dry martinis on birthdays. Dad taught me how to make the perfect martini – five parts gin to one-part vermouth. Stir and refrigerate, serve in chilled martini glasses with three olives – two is bad luck.

So, it was a lovely and unexpected thing to enjoy a cocktail with Leslie in Manhattan. When I asked my Dad what he wanted me to do for him over there, the first thing he said was "Find a great jazz bar and order a martini," so I did. It was one of the many things he wanted me to experience over there. The jazz bar was exactly what you would expect – a basement club, dark and dingy (but not smoky), with little round tables and a cool jazz band that Samantha seemed to love. I personally thought it was a bit scatty, but perhaps I don't get jazz.

It always surprises me how easy it is to adapt to a new place so, when the time came to leave New York, our ferry and our wonderful apartment, it was a sad day. I was excited to see my children, but I didn't want to leave. I know my sisters felt the same. Dad says the best time to leave a place is when you want to stay, and I was definitely doing that.

I was looking forward to seeing my father and telling him all our adventures, so I phoned him the moment we arrived in Melbourne.

After all, he was the one who helped make it all happen.

The answer I got was not what I expected.

"Hello love," he answered. "I thought I would have heard from you yesterday."

"No Dad," I said. "We just got back this morning. Remember, it was Thursday we were returning."

"Oh, okay love. Okay. Well I hope you had the best time," he said. "When can I see you? I've missed you love."

My worry radar went up hearing Dad's voice. He sounded strange but I hoped it was nothing and dismissed it as I was still on a high from our fabulous adventure. I was sad it was over and wanted to make sure I found a way of keeping that magical feeling of being in New York with my sisters where anything in the world was possible and life was full of wonder and awe again.

CHAPTER 8

THE CALL THAT CHANGED EVERYTHING

The missed call came at 10pm on Monday. I was being driven home from a dinner date with a guy I'd been out with a few times. I quite liked him but didn't want to seem too eager so thought a Monday night date would be perfect without the intensity of a weekend night. Since my divorce, I had decided it was time to start dating again as the "new, improved me", and see if I could do it with "no expectations, and just for fun" like my friends always suggested.

"You take things too seriously Melissa. Just go out and enjoy yourself. Every man you date doesn't have to be the next husband." So, I was reluctantly giving it a go, and time would tell.

Driving home, I laughed it off when I heard Dad's message saying that we should change the doctor's appointment, which was for 9.45 the next morning. As I got closer to home, I knew I had to call. My Dad is a stickler for time. Always regaling tales of the army when time meant everything, at 87 he still kept to a strict schedule of daily activities. Tonight was different.

Quickly saying goodbye to my date, I raced inside to call my Dad, convinced that there must be some rational explanation. Dad just wouldn't get something like that confused. He's the most level-headed man I know. I decided if Dad asked, I wouldn't tell him I had been on a date. He'd had such high hopes for me, and I felt like I had fallen so short with yet another marriage breakup. The last thing he needed was to be worried about me again so I would just keep it quiet.

As the phone rang, I could feel my pulse beating in my throat. Please answer Dad and please laugh when you do. Then I will know it's all been a big mistake, that life as I know it will go on. That my Dad, my mentor and best friend is still the same. At the worst times in my life with relationship breakups or health scares, my Dad was always at my side. I was just starting to feel put back together from the crying mess I had been for the past year and couldn't stand the idea that something might be wrong with him.

He answered the phone in his usual gruff manner. He loves to hear from his daughters but always sounds like he's been interrupted.

"Hi Dad, its Missy. I just saw a missed call from you."

"Oh yeah love, sorry to bother you but I was thinking we should ring and change the appointment," he answered.

He'd been saying sorry to bother you a lot lately. He was never a bother.

In the background I could hear the radio blaring loudly but distorted as it always does, slightly off the station. Dad only has the radio on during the day while he's sitting in his chair waiting for the afternoon news to come on. That crinkly brown leather recliner with the red pillowcase on the head rest that covers torn fabric is where he spent so many of his days now. His remote controls lined up neatly on the coffee table beside him, the tv guide and glasses case, and the Mensa quiz that he proudly works on every weekend, knowing how important it is to keep mentally active.

"Dad it's okay, the appointment is not until tomorrow. Dad do you know what time it is? Its night-time. It's after 10 at night. Are you okay?"

He said he was fine and just made a mistake, but I knew there was something more. I wished I hadn't drunk wine at dinner, then I could jump straight in my car and check on him. But losing my license a year ago for drink driving after my marriage breakup I was still on 0 alcohol so decided that I would see him in the morning.

My phone lay beside my head as I tried to go off to sleep watching Netflix like I always do. It's funny how you get into a routine when you are alone again. It was me, the cat and Netflix most nights. I found it hard to go to sleep, thinking of my Dad sitting in his chair listening to the radio in the night-time. It wasn't him. This was not his routine. Was he fully dressed? Had he had dinner? What's been going on in his house?

He has always been a man of solitude, an independent soul and deep thinker but the years were taking their toll. He was slowing down but still staunchly self-sufficient and dignified. Continually surprising me with his knowledge and wisdom, he listened to everything and always had an opinion which I often took on as my own. He taught me to question all things.

A country boy at heart, Dad loved his mountains and it was only a couple of years ago during some particularly devastating fires in January, he made the decision to leave his beloved acreage in Romsey and move down to the peninsula to be closer to me. He had even stopped driving his red RX7, which he would take to mass at Woodend and the local shops once a week, knowing his eyesight and reflexes were starting to deteriorate. The move to Mornington was difficult but he had always been sensible and knew that it was time so tried to make the most of it, always true to his philosophy: "It's not what happens to you love, it's how you react to it."

He had only ever lived on the peninsula once before when I was unwell 15 years ago and needed some help from my family. That's how much he loves me. He left his stunning five acres in Woodend, with the wooden swing between two ghost gums, and a view that looked right over Macedon where, at a certain time of day, the sun illuminated the big white cross at the top of the hill, and came to McCrae.

But it was never his home. Like his misplaced furniture and paintings, he just didn't fit there and, once I recovered and he knew it was safe, he quickly returned to his treasured mountain, stating "they're all too old for me down here anyway".

I missed Dads second call that night at 4am, waking up to the phone ringing at 4.05.

"Missy where are you? What time do you think you'll be here love?"

I jumped out of bed and told Dad I was on my way. Panic set in but I still managed to put my lipstick on and freshen my face. I rang the nurse on call who was hopeless, asking banal questions. Who cares if Dad has a cough? How do I know what medicine he's on? And no, I'm not with him. He is all alone and I have to get over there. I hung up from her and called an ambulance that would meet me there.

The air was crisp as I went to my car, still dark but with the anticipation the sun would peep through any minute. There's always something unfamiliar but intriguing about that time of day, a promise of things to come. I realised as I drove too quickly along the back streets of Moorooduc, I am only ever up at this time for extremely good or terribly bad reasons.

Good mornings were driving to the airport for a flight somewhere exciting when you didn't care what time of day it was, and the anticipation was palpable. I had just last week returned from New York with my two sisters on an adventure that my Dad insisted we have.

"Everybody has to see New York at least once in their lifetime," he told me when I was trying to decide if I could afford to go. New York seemed so far away now.

As I pulled into the driveway of the brown stone brick veneer Dad had called home for a year now, the lounge room lights were all on and I wondered what I might find. Before I had a chance to get out of the car, Dad appeared fully dressed with his shopping bag and walking stick ready for our outing.

He was always prepared when I arrived for the weekly shopping visit and met me at the car to save time. I wished it were time to go shopping.

"Hi Dad, it's very early and not time to go yet, let's go inside and sit down."

The scratchy noise from the radio made it hard to concentrate as I tried to explain that he had mixed up the times. He slumped in his chair with a vacant look I had never seen. His shrinking frame melded into the upholstery, concaved like he was becoming part of that piece of furniture that he spent so many hours on. His grey spikey hair was barely visible, but he insisted on having it cut every two weeks. His breathing laboured as he sat there trying to process what I was telling him, and for the first time ever I saw my Dad scared. My eyes scanned the room like a detective looking for clues on the past 24 hours. The tv hadn't been on and I imagined him sitting in that chair and not going to bed at all.

It was at times of crisis I always found I could be the best version of myself. Sitting there with my Dad I realised there was something very wrong and I was determined to get to the bottom of it.

The flashing lights from the ambulance were like a beacon as they pulled into the driveway.

CHAPTER 9

THE BEGINNING OF THE END

The paramedics arrived with all their paraphernalia, two young strapping blokes who both had kindness in their eyes. Dad remained in his chair as they started to ask him questions about what had happened, taking notes on a small notebook and placing the blood pressure cuff around his skinny arm. I'm always in awe of people who choose this profession and can't imagine doing 12-hour shifts, being faced with life and death and the trauma of car accidents or dealing with a grieving family.

"A hell of a way to earn a crust" Dad once commented when we saw an ambulance race by.

I ran around the house trying to find his medication. It made me feel useful until I couldn't find it, but they said not to worry.

It all seemed surreal as I explained to them that Dad had somehow mixed up the times, it was like he couldn't tell the difference between day and night.

Dad insisted that it was all fuss about nothing, but I was glad to see that he was willing to cooperate when they wanted to take him to the hospital for further investigation.

It didn't seem that long ago since Dad was last put in an ambulance, and I wondered if this is a common experience for people when their parents start to get older. Just a few months before, I had been sitting at home one Tuesday night and suddenly had an urge to call. This might not seem strange to most people, but Dad and I had a routine. I would call him Wednesdays after dinner, and he would call me Sunday mornings around 9. It was a way to keep in touch particularly when he was living far away in the country, and it had just stuck.

I had a bad feeling when he didn't answer the phone that night and dialed his number over and over again. It was 8.02 so he should be sitting down in his brown leather chair, watching the ABC. He should have had his dinner, sitting at the end of the table with his red placemat that he and mum had since I was a kid, and then be in his chair, possibly with a glass of red.

I knew that something was wrong so raced over there to find the house unlocked, lights on, and a defrosted chop still sitting in the sink in a crumpled-up plastic bag.

I looked around the house frantically, racing from room to room, to his bedroom and en suite, his spare room and study with the antique roll top desk where he kept all his precious paper work and poems neatly stored, and then outside to see if he had fallen somewhere. I even checked the streets as Dad often goes for a walk along the esplanade, (these days with a walker), but he was nowhere to be seen.

In the meantime, I had called my aunty to see if perhaps he was with her and, luckily, she had phoned all the hospitals to see if he was there.

Sure enough he had been taken to Frankston, so I jumped in the car and headed there.

Dad was shocked when I arrived at the hospital as he was just being taken out of the ambulance and was waiting on the rails with the paramedics. The rails I found out is the place the paramedics line up the stretchers waiting with patients to be seen. I looked around to see the steel rails along the wall, which must be where the name came from.

He had fallen over and hurt his shoulder at home and was being monitored. The paramedics checked their notes and said Dad had been loaded into the ambulance at exactly 8.02pm, and I remembered a life lesson I had learnt recently to always follow your gut instinct.

Driving to the hospital this time was different. My sister was on her way down as soon as she heard. She lives an hour away in Pakenham, but she also sensed there was something very wrong so jumped in her car straight after my call.

Samantha is not an early riser. Working from home as an employment consultant she makes her own hours, but she knew by my tone this was serious.

Walking into the hospital, I could feel the tears welling up in my eyes. I have always believed I can handle everything but never cope well when something is wrong with my Dad. He has always been my rock and now I had to be strong and look after him. I knew if he saw me crying it would just upset him, so I took a deep breath and walked into the emergency department with my head held high.

"Never let them see you hurting" was often Dad's advice and something I had tried to put into practice when I was going through my recent divorce. Whenever I saw my ex-husband, I would be calm and courteous even though inside I wanted to either break down in tears or hit him for what he did.

They had taken Dad into a cubicle and he was sitting next to the bed when I got there. His walking stick, which was never far away from him these days, was leaning against the chair, and a doctor was asking him questions about what had happened.

He didn't seem to comprehend that he had mixed up the times so drastically but admitted that he had been a little bit confused with the days this week.

"I went out to get my paper and it wasn't there on the weekend so I rang and had a go at the newsagent but they said it was Saturday not Sunday and my paper was delivered on Sunday,'' he explained to the doctor, as if he was trying to pass a test. If I give the right answers, they will let me go.

Before long the doctor turned to me and asked me what I thought had happened. How do I explain to a stranger that this man, who is the wisest and most loving person I know, doesn't understand what time or day it is? How do I do that without breaking his heart because he will think I have no faith in him anymore? And that, for this man, who is just another patient to you, dignity is everything.

So, I told him what had happened in the most diplomatic way possible, the late night and early morning phone calls, the confusion with the paper, and what I had noticed about Dad in the last week since I got home.

The seething look from Dad went right through me as I gave my testimony. He was disappointed I was not on his side right now. We were always on each other's side. It was a pact. "Hey what have I told you love? I am the one person in this world you never have to apologise to" was something he always said to me. I don't think he was feeling that now.

A constant stream of patients and visitors, white-coated doctors and nurses scuffled past the paper curtain that separated Dad and I from the world. Alarm bells and a code grey 5C announcement occasionally interrupted the muffled noises across the intercom. Dad and I sat there in limbo, waiting for what we did not know.

When Samantha arrived, she was ready to take control. Even though she is my younger sister, she has always been the 'take charge girl' and is a born fixer. If Dad has a problem with his phone or a bill, he gets straight onto Samantha to sort it out, and often suggests I do the same. She's been able to get Dad refunds on flights, power bills and recently organized a new mobile phone for him with bigger keys as he was having trouble seeing the small ones on his little nokia. She makes DVDs for the family that she tapes off Foxtel and sends them to each of us with a typed synopsis and recommendations of shows we individually might enjoy. Mum gets all the "Young and the Restless" episodes so she can still watch it now it's not on free to air television. Dad gets BBC shows and inspirational, often historical movies, and I get romantic comedies and the odd literature related film.

Today was no different. After kissing Dad and I hello, she wanted to be caught up to speed on where we were at, nodding and saying "aha" to each piece of new information as if she was mentally processing the situation. Then true to form, she pulled out of her purple bag bottles of water and a left-over sandwich just in case we were hungry.

I stared down at that bag on the floor and realised she was finally using the one she had bought in New York. It was a laughing point amongst us three girls that she had bought so many bags and insisted on using her old one while we were away. She smiled at me with the kind of comforting recognition that only two sisters can share.

Dad has always encouraged our unity, writing in one of his first poems to us three girls:

"Do not let the obvious confuse your inner minds
Your differences will only emphasise the loving tie that binds
For you are yourselves and of this you must be proud
But do not let these superficialities true natures love to cloud
Enjoy the very unique things that make you stand apart
While knowing deep inside yourself of the whole you are a part."

The doctors did not know what was going on with Dad, but I had this sinking feeling this was the beginning of the end. It's the kind of feeling when you know in your gut that life as you knew it might never be the same. It probably seems strange for a grown woman to be so melancholy about her Dad. Maybe that's how everyone feels when their parents start to wilt away, and I could see my Dad disappearing in front of my eyes. I also know that I have a tendency for melodrama (a trait I get from my mum) so decided optimism was the way to go and ignore words like stroke and dementia being bandied around in hushed tones by the nurses. "Deal with the facts" Dad would often say. "Define the problem and then find the solution."

So, the facts were Dad would be kept in hospital for further tests and consultations.

CHAPTER 10

AT LEAST WE KNOW HE'S EATING

Dad always had this joke about aged care facilities, referring to them as "maximum security living" but within a few days, he was allowed home as long as someone was with him. That meant my sister and me. The doctors said it wasn't safe for him to be at home until they could assess his mental state, but they had found another problem that had to be dealt with first – an aortic aneurism. All that praying at mass must have paid off, as this was Dad's second aneurism that had been found accidentally. (The first one was 20 years ago when Dad had been complaining of an upset stomach. He was living on his acreage in Woodend by himself and was days away from it rupturing when they discovered it and operated the following day).

So, Samantha and I were the gatekeepers, although my sister's rules were a lot stricter than mine.

"Now remember Missy he's not allowed to drink or smoke. Make sure you don't let him," she had said to me almost concerned to leave me alone with Dad. And she was right. The moment her car left the driveway, Dad was up getting a scotch and a smoke and heading outside. I, of course, joined him, as this is what we did.

When my youngest daughter was living with her Dad for a few months, after I lost my license, I would spend every Tuesday night at

Dads. I called it "Tuesdays with David". He would cook dinner; we would drink wine and smoke cigarettes inside and read his latest poetry. "Well that was a great night," Dad would say. "Once again we solved the problems of the world."

"What harm can one smoke and a drink do?" I thought to myself as Dad and I sat outside that night. "The guy's 87. Let him have this."

I remember when I had been sick all those years ago and doing familiar little things became so important. My friend Lisa used to bring her straightener and makeup to the hospital and do my hair and, for a brief moment, I forgot I was a patient.

For the next three weeks Dad and I would spend every weekend together and Samantha would take over weekdays when I went to work. After spending so many weeks there, she had set the back bedroom up beautifully with a purple lamp (her favourite colour), portable DVD player (again purple), and a lovely dish for our jewellery. There were vases of flowers in the kitchen and lounge that she had either brought or picked from the garden.

We felt like we had fallen down the rabbit hole during those days. Dad was so disoriented (correct spelling, unlike disorientated which I heard people often say) especially at night.

My aunty bought around lots of food, (jarred chops, lemon citrus cake), which we would often have for dinner and Samantha , of course, made incredible meals each labelled in individual containers (chicken risotto, beef stroganoff, pasta marinara) for Dad and I to enjoy.

After the "scotch and smoke" incident, Dad had decided to ask his local doctor, Mohamed Elsweedy (my sister called him "Dr Sweety" after she met him and thought he was totally cute), if he was allowed to drink and smoke. Dr Sweety said definitely not, and so Dad agreed he would refrain for now. Dr Sweety (I had to remind myself not to call him that when addressing him) had been Dad's gp from the time he moved to the peninsula. It's very important for older people to have a good doctor as they spend so much time there. Most of our weeks in the past year had been a calendar of shopping and lunch with intermittent medical appointments.

Dr Sweety, I learnt, is from Egypt and has been practicing over here for fifteen years. Like my sister, he is Muslim. Samantha converted to Islam many years ago much to our Dad's shock. As a staunch Catholic, he found it hard to understand her choice, but time heals everything, and they are good now. I never understood his problem with it, but then I have always been an "each to their own" girl, and love Samantha's capacity for faith and unyielding passion for whatever she sets her heart to.

She has always marched to the beat of her own drum and, even as a young child, was searching for some deeper truth to life. She was way ahead of her time as a teenager, listening to Carol King and burning incense in her room till the wee hours of the morning.

So, after dinner with no alcohol, Dad and I would sit down to watch one of the movies Samantha had taped. We had our routine. Dad would sit in his brown leather chair and I had the faded tan recliner that had travelled from our family home in Bulleen to Woodend, McCrae, Romsey and now Mornington. It was part of the settlement when he and mum got divorced, along with the olive-green chairs and extendable dining table.

His lounge room is filled with treasures of a life well lived – a tiny replica of the concord which he got when he took its final flight, a bust of Tutankhamen from his trip to Egypt, New Guinea artefacts he put together on a display board, and majestic paintings by his brother Ian. A bookshelf that reaches to the ceiling houses his favourite writers - Banjo Paterson, Henry Lawson, and Cervantes' Don Quixote with whom he has a particular affiliation.

Most nights, when we sat in that room, Dad fell asleep in front of the movie and rarely saw one to the end. Often, he would get out of his chair thinking it was over and say, "That was great love. I really enjoyed that."

I didn't have the heart to tell him he'd been asleep the whole time so just agreed. Then every night, without fail, he would put on his pyjamas and come out without his teeth to say goodnight.

With everything that I witnessed in those three weeks, that was the most disconcerting. Samantha and I later laughed about it to the point of crying in that way that only something truly sad can be that funny.

I understand now why elderly people become like children as I had to keep alert just in case Dad woke up. It reminded me of when my babies were little, listening out for their cries. This time I was listening out for Dad getting up in the middle of the night. Most nights I would wake to the smell of toast cooking and come out to see him fully dressed sitting at the table with his red placemat eating his breakfast at 2 in the morning.

"Morning love, would you like a coffee?"

"Um Dad, it's not time for breakfast yet. It's still the middle of the night."

"Oh shit, I've done it again haven't I? I'll go back to bed then. Sorry love."

At first it was heartbreaking, but as the weeks went on, Samantha and I got used to it. We put notes on the doors and chairs against them telling Dad not to leave. It felt disrespectful to be treating him like this, but we were both concerned for his safety. I didn't know if the notes were necessary but hoped that, amongst all his confusion, Dad didn't know. Deep down I knew he did. I could see the disappointment in his eyes every time he got up at the wrong time. Sometimes I would wake up three times during the night to toast being cooked. Samantha and I laughed, "At least we know he's eating."

CHAPTER 11

MAXIMUM SECURITY LIVING

After weeks of living with Dad (and him having to live with us), we finally had a hospital date. Dad had grown accustomed to having a bag packed just in case we had to go to hospital and so his tan leather overnight bag was ready and waiting at the front door. He would go to Frankston hospital and then be taken to a rehabilitation place to assess his mental state. A social worker had been around and asked lots of questions to test his cognitive skills. This seemed pointless to me. He could answer questions about general knowledge better than either of us but was still mixing up the days, so clearly there was something not right. I had never thought of my Dad as elderly but had started to see signs of deterioration over the past year. He was struggling walking at times, so we went and bought a walking frame for when he does his esplanade walk to see "his horizon". Dad had insisted a year ago that, if he was to leave his beloved mountains, he had to have a horizon close by, and Port Phillip Bay was the next best thing. He loves his horizons so much he wrote a poem devoted to them:

"In a vast land like Australia, horizons stretch beyond the eye
But over desert lands and oceans, dawn will fill the sky
The glorious colour of the sun, paints waves of sand and sea

Chase the shadows of our earth, just for you and me."

The vascular surgeon had decided to do a less invasive operation so Dad would not be cut open. He would have keyhole surgery to repair the aneurism, and it is much less dangerous.

Dr Chris Brown was much younger than I expected. Sitting there beside Dad's hospital bed, vaguely listening to the information he was telling Dad about the surgery, it occurred to me that some people do achieve great success in their lives. I couldn't help reflecting on my own life and thinking about all the time I must have wasted. It's not that I have a lot of regrets. I have four beautiful children and a granddaughter who I adore. I love my job as a journalist (well feature writer in truth) but I have wasted a lot of time searching for the perfect relationship. I realised I could have been putting that time to good use and wondered if this doctor also had a good personal life as well as a great career.

Before we knew it, Dad was being wheeled away. No muss, no fuss. Just gone. Samantha and I sat in the ward where the bed once was and decided to go and see a movie. This might seem insensitive, but the nurses had told us he would be in theatre for at least four hours, so we checked out the cinemas close by and headed down there.

Boy did we choose the wrong film to take our mind off our Dad. I can't remember what it was called but the father in it died from an operation at which point Samantha and I both nervously checked our phones and willed for the movie to be over.

When we got back to the hospital, Dad still hadn't returned. They sent us down to the waiting room outside ICU as that is where he would be taken after recovery. The ICU waiting room is a scary place to be, like how I imagined purgatory to be when the catholic priest at primary school would march around the classroom telling us it was the place between heaven and hell. I was already a nervous kid, and this terrified me and made me determined never to go there. (Surprisingly, once I became a boy crazy teenager, I ended up doing everything that might land me there, but I had forgotten all about it by then).

Dad came through the surgery with flying colours. He was still attached to machines when we were finally allowed in there, but it was a textbook procedure and he should recover well according to the doctors.

Samantha and I should have been happy with this news, but both still had a sense of doom. The doctor had also said that Dad's confusion would most likely get worse after the operation and we didn't know what we were in for when he started recovering.

The hospital was horrendous, and Dad was taken to a ward with elderly patients that looked a whole lot sicker than him. The four-bed ward smelt of stale urine and the people there were terminally ill. The lady to Dad's right looked of European descent and slept a lot during the day. Her bed was surrounded by vases of flowers in all shapes and colours, so I immediately raced down to buy Dad flowers too. His little area looked so unloved, but so did he. He didn't want to get out of bed. He didn't even want to watch the tv. He just lay there like he was giving up. We did encourage him to play a few hands of gin rummy and he still managed to beat me, which wasn't unusual. I had always been terrible at games. But I was worried about him. I have seen people will themselves to death before when they get terminal illness. Mums friend Noreen Conroy was a tall, elegant woman who, at 45, was diagnosed with bowel cancer. Her spirit disappeared and she died within two weeks. Dad's health wasn't terminal, but his spirit was.

"I just want to go home love. I hate it here" he said to me. It did occur to me that maybe I should just grab a wheelchair and make a run for it. I'd watched a movie recently where the daughter (Hilary Swank) takes her father (Robert De Nero) out of the hospital on New Year's Eve to see the ball drop in Times Square, and he just loves it. But I couldn't see our script going that well, so we made a joke about it and played another hand of cards.

After a couple of weeks Dad was given the medical clearance to go to the rehab facility. The doctor was happy with his progress and now it was onto stage two.

We packed up his belongings and met him at "The Mornington", a medical centre for elderly people. It was just a few minutes from my work at the paper and quite a modern looking building. It looked like it had been architecturally designed to fit with the native landscape with its wooden slatted walls, exposed beams and plenty of glass. As I walked further towards the front entrance, I thought it looked more like a gallery than a rehabilitation place.

Inside was pristine, with a receptionist at the front desk behind a glass divider, who smiled kindly when I walked in, and asked if I needed any help.

"My father, David Carr, has just been transferred here from Frankston Hospital."

"No problem dear, I will check what ward he's on."

I loved it when older people called me dear. There's nothing like hanging round an older generation to make you feel young.

"Your father is on level 3, bed 9," she said, and handed me a tiny ticket with four numbers on it.

"You will need to use that when you leave."

I didn't know what the numbers were for but looking around the place I thought, "This doesn't look too bad". I loved the modern flower arrangements, potted plants, and paintings by local artists on the walls. There was a small café downstairs with a couple of steel tables and chairs, and a bain marie with pies and sausage rolls. Behind the counter was an older looking lady in a pink uniform with perfectly coiffured hair, serving coffee and tea, and a lovely assortment of homemade lamingtons and iced vovo biscuits, who pointed me to the direction of the elevator.

CHAPTER 12

WE'RE NOT IN KANSAS ANYMORE

The spacious lift took me up to level 3 where my father would be staying for the next few weeks.

By this stage I had already lost the piece of paper with the numbers but wasn't concerned as I had entered the lift with no problem. It hadn't occurred to me that I needed a code to leave.

I looked for Dad amongst elderly people with walking frames who could barely keep their shaky body upright, and room after room filled with lost souls staring at the television or, worse, at nothing. I was at once terrified at what I might find and determined that my father would not become one of the forgotten generation. I had interviewed many old people over my career as a journalist and was always blown away by their inspirational stories. Women who had served in the army long before the feminist movement or stayed behind and raised a family while their husbands were at war. Men who had spent six decades serving in the fire brigade, witnessing tragedy I couldn't fathom. I was certain these residents at 'The Mornington' were no different and it broke my heart to see living treasures in such despair. I understood that a lot of them might have severe dementia and, perhaps, not even know their own name, but it was a real eye opener that this place was just minutes from where I worked every day, and I had no idea.

Dad was sitting in a chair beside the window when I got to his room. His clothes had already been put away in the drawers and the skinny wooden wardrobe beside the bed. There was a tv anchored high on the ceiling and a white board with his name and the name of his carer in large, bold letters.

There was a huge clock on the wall next to the whiteboard with clearly distinct numbers.

Dad was eating a hot lunch of hamburger with gravy; some mashed potatoes and vegetables and barely looked up when I walked in. Food was one of the few pleasures he had these days and I had noticed how much he loves his meals whenever we were together.

I looked at Dad and wished we were enjoying a meal at our favourite winery "10 Minutes by Tractor", a two chef's hat restaurant where the waiter always gave us the same table in the corner near the fireplace and made a fuss of Dad every time we went there.

"I wonder what the poor people are doing?" Dad would say as we toasted our champagne and enjoyed the delight of whatever special occasion we were celebrating. "Remember darling the world is beautiful, life is sweet."

I couldn't see the same light in Dad's eyes anymore and wondered if his joie de vivre was still there. I've spent enough time in hospitals to know how hard it is to stay positive, but Dad has always taught the importance of mentally overcoming what is physically happening to you. If the idea that he was not as strong mentally was freaking me out, imagine what it was doing to him. He sat there and stared out the window, like a man giving in to his fate, his lunch tray in front of him, a folded-up newspaper corner peeking out from underneath the unbalanced tray.

"It's a beautiful day out there, Dad" I said, trying to small talk my way out of the awkward silence. For in that silence was the truth my father talked about.

"So, hold this thought despite the times

That I may appear aloof
And look within this aching heart
For the silent burning truth."

There was only one other time I can remember when Dad and I experienced the uncomfortable silence. I was 18 and pregnant with my first child, and Dad didn't cope. I had disappointed him and all the dreams for the future he had for his eldest daughter. Living at home while I was pregnant, Dad did his best to ignore the growing belly. I had broken his heart and I knew it. As a strict catholic, and ex-army man, our upbringing was regimented, and this was not the path he expected for his girl.

Thirty years later, as we sat in the hospital room, the silence was the same. Life was not taking the turn either of us had expected, and neither of us knew how to cope.

You know how people say "be careful what you wish for", well for me it was about to come true when Dad broke the silence by saying "the thing that gets me the most about this is you don't have any faith in me anymore."

The words hung in the air like a knife.

"That's not fair Dad. I do have faith in you and always have. Yes, I'm worried about you and don't understand what's going on. I'm just as confused as you are. I've stood up for you this whole time. Every time someone questions you, I tell them how clever you are, and I hope this is just a passing phase. I just want you to be back home where you belong."

By this stage I was crying but Dad couldn't see it. I'm not sure if it was his failing eyesight or the fact that he was so angry and self-involved that he couldn't see how upset I was. Later when I told my daughter Vicky what had happened, she put it into perspective.

"Grandfather must be so scared now mum. He doesn't know what is happening to him and he is just lashing out."

She was right and I remembered all the times when the kids were teenagers and took out their frustrations on me, knowing that I was the one person in the world that would never leave them no matter how hideous they were. I decided that now Dad needed that too.

That night I got a phone call from Dad, apologising for what he said and explaining how much he was hating this and didn't mean to take it out on me. From then on there were no more awkward silences between us.

Three weeks later my Dad was allowed to leave. He was to go back home, and the council would organise extra services to help him live an independent life. My sister and I couldn't believe it. His confusion and disorientation had gone, and our lives would return to normal. The doctors couldn't explain what had happened to Dad, why he had been so confused and why he was getting up in the middle of the night, but they said he was capable of living independently and that was good enough for me. It had been a long road and it had taken its toll on him. He just wanted to get home, so we packed up the car with his bags, and a new shower seat that Samantha had organised, and left the car park. It had been three months and Dad breathed a sigh of relief as we drove through the steel gates to his freedom.

Within a couple of weeks, we had our new routine.

Dad and I would meet up every second Sunday to go to mass and then lunch at our new favourite place "Manhattan" where the owner there had taken an instant like to my father.

He had an uncanny resemblance to her own father whom she had lost a couple of years ago and had a black and white photograph of him on her wall that she insisted showing me.

He was refined and dignified like my Dad, who always dressed immaculately for church and our lunches with his Panama hat and trench coat.

"Treasure this time with your father," she said to me, but I already did.

CHAPTER 13

A BOTTLE OF WINE AND A MOBILE PHONE

One Saturday night, I was alone on the couch (not unusual). After a couple of glasses of red (okay a bottle!) I saw an advertisement on the television saying they were taking new applications for a reality tv show, Married at First Sight. My daughter, Lizzy and I had been watching the current season and it became a regular bonding session for us. When you find something you can share with your 15-year-old you don't say no! My daughter and I got on well but had the usual problems a mother has with a teenager and this was the first thing we had really enjoyed together for a long time. Normally our nights went like this – me making dinner and watching tv on the couch; Lizzy in her room watching YouTube videos. Occasionally, we mixed it up and she watched YouTube videos on the couch next to me.

This particular night I was alone. Lizzy had gone to stay at a friend's house, and I was having a night in (not a shock. I quite enjoyed my own company now and wasn't desperate to go out and party or date every weekend. This was all part of my version of doing things differently. "It's all about balance" as my father often said).

Before I knew it, I had downloaded the application form on my phone and was applying. I couldn't download the Telstra app but this I could do!! Go figure!!

I filled out my name, age, and location and pages of questions that wanted graphic detail about my personal life and relationship history. It wasn't pretty. The more I filled out, the more I realised how busy I had been. Two marriages, several relationships, four children, one granddaughter, renting now, dating occasionally, don't trust my own judgement, yep that was me in a nutshell.

Next to upload some photos but which ones? I wanted to give an accurate view of my life but also show I was fun, and a young at heart grandma who enjoyed travelling. Let's leave out the pics that reflect me crying alone in my room, ridden with anxiety about the bad choices I have made – they don't need to see those. Photos of me in New York outside Tiffany, and in central park, a couple of a Day on the Green to show I could still rock an outdoor concert, and photos with my granddaughter seemed perfect. And to finish off a five-minute video answering these questions. What is your name and age? How many relationships have you had? What went wrong in the main ones? What would you like to have in your ideal relationship? What is your personality like? Why do you need us to help you find love?

I went upstairs to my room, sat on the floor and started my video.

"My name is Melissa Walsh and I am 53 years of age, have been married twice and have made VERY bad decisions with men."

What did I want and what went wrong with the others? Now, this was something to really think about.

"I want a partner who loves and accepts me and doesn't try to change me. I want someone into art and literature and travel. I definitely don't want someone younger, but I want them to be young at heart. And what happened in the past? That's easy. I settled for less than I deserve."

So that was it – I uploaded the video, finished the bottle of wine and went off to bed, but not before I deleted the video first to avoid embarrassment.

Not giving it another thought, I went on with my usual life – going to work at the magazine, looking after Lizzy, the occasional date. I am one of those people who don't always listen to my messages, so it is no surprise that the message from the producer was on my message bank for a week before I heard it.

"Hi Melissa, this is Amy from Married at First Sight. Could you please call us back regarding your application?"

I nearly fell off my chair. I listened to the message several times. Yes, she definitely said Married at First Sight. Oh my God!

I summoned up the courage to phone back and leave a message and a youthful sounding girl called me back straight away.

"Hi Melissa, we received your application and would like to talk to you about it further. We are very interested in finding out more about you."

She asked if I had skype (which I didn't) and told me how to install it so we could have a face to face skype interview the next day at 2pm.

I came home from work on my lunch break and didn't tell a soul. I wasn't quite sure what I had done but felt like it was a bit of an adventure. At the very least, it was something to do. And perhaps they could find someone perfect for me. I certainly hadn't done well by myself, and definitely didn't trust my own judgement anymore.

I set up the laptop on my bed and waited for her call. I was so nervous. What was I doing? I tried not to give it too much thought and answer the questions she asked me with complete honesty.

That was easy to do. A year after the disastrous marriage, I had become accustomed to brutal honesty with myself. It was the only way to heal and try to make sure I didn't repeat the same mistakes.

I told her all about myself – the good and the bad. I didn't trust my judgement. I was devastated that I had made such bad choices with men. I wanted my children to see me in a good relationship for once.

If I wanted to have someone really see me for who I am, I had to not be afraid to be myself. I knew who that was now. I had been lost for years, desperate to have someone love me. Now I didn't need it, but it would be nice.

You do get tired of going to things by yourself when you see friends and family in loving and supportive relationships. I had done that for years. In between disastrous breakups (and there were many), I went to events alone and I got used to it.

I had started to think that maybe the universe was trying to tell me that a relationship just wasn't for me, but perhaps I could give this a go.

The skype chat ended, and I went back to work, again not giving it another thought. The following week I received an email with more questionnaires to fill out. I was through to the third stage, and the questions were becoming more personal.

Number of partners, sexual history, number of one night stands, longest time in between relationships, most recent relationship, did I want children (that didn't apply), exactly what I like in a partner physically – age, height, weight, hair colour (if they have hair), etc.

One question got me however – When was the last time I was in love?

"In love?" I thought. "In Love."

I had always thought I knew what being in love would feel like. I thought I would know the moment I met the right person, as if it would hit me like a bolt of lightning. Perhaps I was naïve. Perhaps I had watched too many romantic comedies or taken all the love poetry I read too seriously. The fact was, I didn't feel like I had ever been 'in love'. I had loved of course. I loved my first husband very much. We were teenagers when we met, had our family together, our first home, and lots of great times. It was definitely love but not the 'head over heels, crazy for you' love I wanted.

So, I told them "I have never been in love."

I'm not sure if that was the clincher but it was the truth, and I soon received an email saying that I was chosen to 'audition'. Audition? Oh my God, now it was getting serious.

It was all strictly confidential – the place, the time, the production house.

I was to drive to Toorak and go to the third floor where Endomol Shine would be in room 244. I was not to tell a soul and definitely not tell anyone who asked me what I was auditioning for.

It's funny. I took that very seriously and, as I walked into the hotel room, a man stopped me and said, "What's going on in there?" Endomol Shine had a big sign out the front "Auditions this way." I replied nervously "I'm not sure, they have just asked me to come in for a meeting."

After signing more paperwork, signing confidentiality agreements and waiting for the next stage, I was then called in to the panel.

I was wearing my favourite purple heels, a black skirt and off the shoulder white top and I immediately felt comfortable when the producer who called me in said "Love the shoes."

I sat down on a chair in the middle of the room, in front of a panel of six people, the executive producer, Tara, the head of Channel nine John Walsh and others who I'm not sure where they fitted in. There were two cameras on me, a lighting and audio man and the questions started being fired.

Cutting straight to the chase, Tara said "Why do you want to go on Married at First Sight?"

It seemed like a strange question. I didn't want to be on a show. I hadn't really thought about it that way. I wanted to have an adventure and possibly find someone.

I told her the same thing I had written in all those questionnaires.

"I have been married twice; I have had lots of relationships but never ever been in love. I have made bad choices with men and I didn't trust my own judgement. I was embarrassed that I had done this in front of my children and wanted them to see me in a good relationship. And maybe having them match me with someone might be the answer."

There's something therapeutic about saying it over and over again, examining your choices, and getting real with yourself. It's like it really sinks in – who you are, how you operate and what you would like for your future.

My Dad says, "If you don't have a clear goal, there's a lot of roads there." I know that is true. I had never really thought about what I wanted until now. I had never loved myself enough to take my own needs and wants into account. Thanks to Bruno and losing everything, I now had no choice. Hopefully the road I was on now would lead me to something real.

I drove home from the audition feeling happy with what I had said. I would have been satisfied if that was as far as it went but, before I knew it, more questionnaires were being emailed through. I was then through to the fifth stage. A producer phoned me and wanted to talk about my family life now. Could I leave to go away for a while at a moment's notice? Do I have any responsibilities to take care of if I was chosen? Well of course I had my daughter Lizzy who still lived with me. I had a full-time job that I didn't want to lose. And my daughter Vicky had just found out she was pregnant with her second child. So yes, I did have some issues to sort out if I was chosen.

It all seemed so surreal, even when I got the phone call saying I was 100 per cent through.

Driving along one day with Lizzy and I remember exactly where we were, in Baxter about to pull into the service station to get fuel when my mobile phone rang.

"It's Erin from Endomol Shine, I have some great news. You are going to go on Married at First Sight."

What the hell? I didn't know whether to be happy or freak out, so I decided it was fine to be both.

The problem was I hadn't told my children or my father much about it. I had laughingly said I applied to the kids but certainly didn't expect it to get this far.

As usual, my children were amazing. My son Daniel who lives in Darwin, had never watched it but his wife loved the show. Vicky thought it was fantastic and Antoinette said, "As long as I'm not mentioned, I support you."

As for my baby girl, Lizzy, she was excited at first then when reality sunk in, it was scary. We both knew I might be away for a week or several months according to how the 'relationship' was going.

Telling my father was nearly as bad as telling him I was pregnant at 18.

I went over to Dad's house in Mornington and we sat in our usual spots in the lounge room – Dad in his recliner with the leather foot stool and me in the old Jason recliner with the cigarette burns in the arms.

"Dad I've got something to tell you," I summoned up the courage to say.

"Yes, love what is it?" he said, not seeming too worried yet.

"Have you heard of a show on channel nine called Married at First Sight? Well I kind of applied for it and was accepted. What do you think Dad? I don't know what to do."

My father's reaction was completely unexpected.

"That's the show where two strangers shack up, right?" he asked, which made me laugh.

Dad had a way of cutting through the bullshit and getting straight to the point.

"Ah yes I guess it is." I said, amused at my father's succinct way of describing it.

"Well hell love. How could you not?" he said.

Dad went on to say that this kind of opportunity doesn't come along every day. He was all for adventures and said this is just like deciding to go to New York. If it's put in front of you, you do it. So that was it. I was going to marry a total stranger and put my faith in the hands of some psychologists in Sydney.

CHAPTER 14

KEEPING IT REAL

My father had two pieces of advice for me before I went off on my adventure.

They were words I lived by and helped me get through a surreal process with my dignity intact. He said to me the day I told him about it: "Okay there is a couple of things I need you to do for me love."

I sat there with bated breath. I always took my father's advice very seriously.

"Now listen carefully," he said as he leaned in. "Be yourself and enjoy every moment."

This was the type of thing my father was famous for – the gems of wisdom that would always turn out to be for my own good.

I took his words of advice with me the entire time, from staying in the hotel room the night before the wedding, to the 5am wake up call for the hairdresser, makeup artist and camera crew to the couple of months filming in Sydney.

I was determined to keep it real for my Dad.

And I know that he enjoyed every moment too. It was great to be able to share it with him, and I think it gave him a renewed zest for life, as he went along the journey with me. It would be our last 'hoorah' that we could share together.

When we arrived at the wedding venue and the big white limousine came to a standstill, I knew my Dad was with me all the way. I knew, if he was there, I could get through anything. We walked down the long grassy hill and Dad, in his eighties, held onto me so I didn't fall, just like he had my entire life.

When my Dad said, "you've got this, love." I knew I could do anything.

The wedding day was a blur, it had started so early and was a whirlwind and I thought John was just lovely. When I got to the end of the aisle and he turned around, my first words were "What the fuck! I know you."

And we all laughed, which turned out to be the best thing.

We immediately bonded over cigarettes. I loved a smoke at the end of the day but stuck to one, and he smoked all the time which I didn't mind. We both had a very easy-going nature and loved being sociable so that was a plus, and we had grown up children (apart from my Lizzy.)

Within hours, we had a great banter going and I felt comfortable straight away. This wasn't a total stranger. I had seen him on the season before when Lizzy and I used to have our 'Married at First Sight' nights. He had been matched with Deb who didn't like him at all. She wanted someone Polynesian apparently.

I didn't want a Polynesian necessarily. I just wanted someone nice.

He and I would continue to laugh and have fun for the next two months. We went to New Zealand together, moved into the apartment in Sydney and met all the others which was fantastic fun. When we walked into the first dinner party, it was like he was a celebrity. Everybody knew him and they were lovely to me too.

We were all in the same boat, on this crazy ride where our lives were taken out of our hands. I personally think it is a bond that will last forever and am still good friends with some of the girls from the show.

I made sure I was always myself but was very careful to not do anything that might embarrass my children (perhaps that ship had sailed even being on the show!) Regardless, it was like they were my moral compass. And John used to say to me "Don't drink too much at the dinner parties, Missy. They will film every negative thing they can."

You quickly get used to terms like "voxy" and "rolling" and "cut" after months of filming reality tv.

And our little cast was like a family, even though we were all different ages, different backgrounds and socio-economic groups.

John and I were the oldest. In fact, I was the first 'grandmother' they had on the show which I found hilarious.

I have never had a problem with admitting my age. I figure it's better to be getting old than the alternative. So, I was happy to be like a surrogate mother to some of the younger girls.

We all stuck together as much as we could and in the early weeks would hang out with each other in our rooms. We had what's app groups which is how we would communicate – Mafs girls and Mafspeeps where constant conversations and photos would pop up to help amuse us in this surreal situation, we were all in. A huge party would soon put all that to a stop. It was the week I was away, and John was alone in our apartment. A heap of the cast had a party in one of their rooms which got a little out of hand. (John slept through it which I thought was hilarious.) Needless to say, the executive producer was soon laying down the law and a curfew was put in place. We all had to be in the room by 8pm. No fraternising with the other cast members and we were to sign in if you go out. I found all of that hilarious. I was 53 for goodness sake. I couldn't remember the last time I had a curfew, but we still did the right thing. If we went out, we made sure we were back by 8 and signed in with our minder, Sheree, who was staying on the next floor down.

Our apartments were on two floors of the Haywood Suites in Sydney, looking right out over the Harbour Bridge and Opera House. It was stunning. Floor to ceiling windows in the bedroom and living area overlooked this 180-degree view. I had never stayed anywhere like it, let alone live there.

But there was a price to pay and, while I had a lot of fun, it was very difficult being away from my children and my Dad.

My daughter Vicky was about to give birth to her second child, and it was very important for me to be there.

The producers could not have been better when we found out Vicky was in labour. It was about 9 o'clock at night and, unlike the other cast, I was allowed to have my phone on set during a dinner party. Nassar was up doing his usual thing, taking centre stage at the dining table and we were all laughing and drinking, having become completely oblivious to the twelve surrounding cameras on rails that framed the full length of the dining room table.

I felt my phone buzz and there was a message from Steve, Vicky's partner. "Melissa just letting you know Vicky is in labour."

I jumped up out of my chair, amongst all the chatter of the dinner party (they tended to get loud as, due to the curfew, we only got to see each other once or twice a week and had a lot to catch up on.)

The producers could not have been nicer, and Tara came out straight away and said we will organise a flight home for you tonight.

My little mafs family were so excited for me. It was actually lovely to be able to share it with them and I promised them I would keep them posted when the baby was born.

John and I headed down the elevator in the warehouse where we did all the filming for the dinner parties and commitment ceremonies every week. We would be driven in a black limousine with a camera crew in front every time, but this time was different. I was loaded into a cab to go back to Melbourne and he would stay in Sydney.

It was strange saying goodbye. I had become used to our little routine in Sydney and our lovely harbour apartment, but I was so excited to go home and see my children and have some alone time too.

It felt like I was living two lives though. There was the one up in Sydney which I had grown accustomed to, but I had my real life at home with my family.

When I arrived home in Melbourne, a car met me at the airport to go back to my townhouse in Hastings. I was to pick Lizzy up on the way through and we would stay back at home until Vicky had her baby.

It was six days before she gave birth, so I looked after my granddaughter, Amy, who is the light of my life. I quickly got back to routine, as if I had never left. Taking Lizzy to school, doing the shopping, hanging out with Amy.

Amy and I had breakfast in bed every morning on the wooden tray I had brought back from Thailand and I loved it. I couldn't have been further away from reality tv, filming and my surreal life in Sydney. She and I would put the laptop on and watch scary movies and then dance around the lounge room. It felt so good being home, but I knew I had to go back and was partly missing being up in Sydney and the life there.

Then the phone call came from Steve: "Vicky had the baby at 3am this morning. They are both doing well. It's a baby girl and her name is Stephanie."

Lizzy and I went to visit Vicky in the hospital the same day, after dropping Amy back with her Dad.

The producers had asked me to film walking into the hospital and talk to the camera about how I was feeling having a new granddaughter.

"You can't escape voxys" they said laughingly.

As Lizzy and I walked into the hospital, I became acutely aware of how bizarre the whole thing was. Here was my beautiful daughter who had just given birth to a baby girl (in my mind, the most 'real' thing a person can do), and here was her mother on hiatus from filming a reality show. The enormity of it hit me as I walked into the room and saw Vicky sitting by the bed with her precious bundle of joy.

This was what life was all about and, once again, I was given the gift of being catapulted back to reality.

The following day, the producers and John were back in town.

We had to film the next episode which was going to be a 'family' meeting – my Dad, Lizzy, and me with John's daughters, one of whom they had flown over from London, which he was thrilled about.

I got to spend one last night in my home and then back up to Sydney, but it had been a wonderful break for me being back with my family. Although I was looking forward to seeing the others and telling them all about my new baby granddaughter.

CHAPTER 15

WHAT'S LOVE GOT TO DO WITH IT?

Stephanie was born on November 6 and little did I know, we would only have three more weeks of filming before we got to come home.

One of the things about doing a reality show is they keep you in the dark about dates, times and where you will be. They want your reactions to be authentic. Each night we received an email telling us the schedule for the next day. Some days it would be a camera crew coming in at 5am to film you waking, other days you might not start until mid-afternoon. So, we were all surprised when we realised we would be home by late November.

The final weeks were becoming more intense with less couples. Every commitment ceremony, someone left until there was only five left. We had become very close by this stage in only the way extreme circumstances can cause people to bond.

John and I were quite tired in the last weeks. At least I had had a break and some down time, but he had stayed up there the week I was away, so he was looking forward to it being over and getting back home to his friends and routine.

He had a big social network and, like me, couldn't wait to do the everyday things he had missed out on during our mafs time – bridge on Fridays, Saturday barbecues with his friends, footy and cricket.

There was a sense of both excitement and doom at the thought of leaving. We had become indoctrinated into this life and it would take some time to get used to life in the outside world again. I knew when we got home, things would be different and I sensed that, in those few short months, I had changed.

There had been a few times during the filming that I had thought to leave. Lizzy was struggling without me and I wanted to get home to her, but it was clear that was not going to happen. I figured I had made my choice to be there, so I had to see it through. It did make me realise that, even if I wanted to, it was going to be hard to leave though and so John and I started referring to it as "Hotel California – You can check out, but you are never going to leave". We laughed about that a lot.

I knew there was only a few weeks to go now and figured we had lasted this long, so why not see it out?

So, our funny little life continued along for the next few weeks – filming commitment ceremonies and dinner parties, where the table settings got less and less, heading off to the casino for a bit of a flutter on our nights off, and watching copious amounts of Netflix in our apartment.

Then came the day we were to leave. I would be filmed walking out the door and down the hallway with John seeing me off. We would then not see each other for a few days until the final 'vow renewal' which would be filmed in a beautiful scenic spot in the Blue Mountains.

We were both flying home to Melbourne to 'talk' to our families about whether we were going to continue with the relationship. It would all be filmed, of course.

I spoke to my daughter Vicky, my father, and my good friend Penny, while John sought advice from his mates and daughter.

The day came for the vow renewal and I was whisked off to NSW again and then the long journey to the Blue Mountains venue. It was so exciting knowing we were on the home straight and that life would soon return to normal.

We had both decided to 'stay' and see how things went in the real world but had to tell each other in the romantic setting for our final episode. Our journey had started in a beautiful park and this is where it would finish, beside a lake, surrounded by flowers and water lilies. When we wrote our final vows, they had to be sent through to the producers for approval. They were happy with mine except for one thing. They asked me if I would say "John, I have fallen in love with you." I laughed when I saw this. It wasn't that I didn't like him, but I had waited fifty years to feel in love and was pretty sure this wasn't it, so I said "I adore him" which was true.

When filming was over, we wandered up to our room and headed out to the local pub for a parma and wine. It was strange sitting there with him, knowing this would be the last time we would be here. I didn't know what would happen when we returned but felt that we would always have a wonderful memory and I was grateful that he was the person I had shared that experience with.

I always thought John was a lovely man. He was kind and generous, but I still felt like I wasn't 'in love'. And so, as I had expected, the connection faded, and another one bit the dust. Would I ever find love? Was I expecting too much? Or was I simply destined to spend the rest of my life alone?

CHAPTER 16

LIVING THE DREAM

Andy Warhol stated, "Everyone will be famous for 15 minutes". That was in 1968 and, as one who has had their brief time in the spotlight, I must tell you it is the strangest thing. One minute you are driving your child to school, paying bills, and putting loads of washing on, the next a car is being sent for you at 5am to do a Today Show link at Channel Nine in Melbourne.

The truth is I hadn't realised the hype surrounding the show until the first commercials started coming out.

Lizzy and I were at home one day when I suddenly heard my own voice saying – "I have made very bad decisions with men." I put down the tea towel and walked over to the television. And there I was, telling the whole world about my hideous love life.

"Meet Married at First Sight's first grandmother, Melissa," the voiceover said.

Lizzy raced out of her bedroom and we both stood there in shock. What had I done? I thought to myself. Suddenly, a wave of anxiety swept over me.

I was home getting back into my normal life again, but I knew everything was about to change. We had finished filming a couple of months before when we reunited in Sydney to film the reunion and do a media tour.

The publicity reps from Channel Nine were constantly emailing, making sure I was still going to be available for interviews and photo shoots when our wedding aired the following Sunday night.

"Yes, I can make myself available for radio interviews and yes I can fly to Sydney to do The Today Show and Talking Married," I remember saying, all the time feeling a sense of uneasiness.

I know we had been away filming for months, but how was I going to be portrayed? When I took my contract to a lawyer before doing the show, I felt like I was signing away my life for the next year. Once you do this, the production company have the rights to use your words and image any way they want. This I knew, but just started to think about it now.

"Pretty sure that horse has bolted" my Dad said to me when I voiced my concerns. "Don't you dare worry, love. You did what I suggested – you were yourself and enjoyed every moment, right?"

Of course, Dad was right. I had enjoyed the entire experience so why should I worry now? Besides, there was nothing I could do about it. I just had to wait and see.

As it turns out, they had portrayed John and I in a beautiful way. We were one of the 'love stories' of the show and, compared to the others, had no real drama at all. In fact, he used to say we were the 'boring couple' which I tried not to be offended about. I think we both came across really well and were totally ourselves which I am still proud of to this day.

What was bizarre was the sudden bombardment of attention once the show aired. John had told me about being recognised but I had no idea what that would be like. He had already had an experience with it the previous year. Even though he and Deb didn't last more than a week, he became a celebrity overnight. Even when we went to the airport to go on our mafs 'honeymoon', the lady at the counter recognised him.

"Oh my god," she said. "You're the guy from that show!"

He looked at her like "Yes it's me" as if this kind of thing happened on a regular basis.

Suddenly, it was me in the spotlight, invited to parties and restaurants, events and balls. I loved it when we all got dressed up to go to charity events and Vicky helped me choose a gorgeous designer dress which you can hire online. When you do a reality show, you tend to lose weight so, after dropping a few kilos, I was feeling very trim and glamorous in that black, slinky dress. John and I had to attend events together which was fine. We actually got on great and I always enjoyed seeing him.

Strangers would come up wanting photos of us, and I was even asked for my autograph. It was odd, but I loved it. At the same time, I knew it wouldn't last and the life I was living in reality was a far cry from the one portrayed.

Fame is very seductive, but it's not real. I do understand how people get sucked into the vortex though. Once you have had a taste of attention, you want more. I've seen it so often now after doing our show and it still makes me sad seeing lovely people in real life who have been entranced over to the 'dark side', doing anything to stay in the spotlight for one more moment.

"You can start to believe your own publicity," my Dad would say. "And that is where the problems begin."

It can happen so easily. Every day you are told things like "Australia's going to love you" and "You guys are the best", so it's bound to have an effect.

Truth is, we are not "Living the dream" as a woman said to me after spotting me in a shopping centre one day. I was used to people stopping me for photos, but this lady took me by surprise. She was so enthusiastic and wanted to believe the hype. "Oh my gosh, life must be amazing for you," she gushed at me. "You're living the dream." I didn't want to tell her the truth, that while the show was great, nothing actually changes. I still have to look after my ageing father, deal with a teenager, pay bills, do housework and grocery shopping. So, I smiled and said "it is awesome. I'm very lucky."

My father always taught me to be grateful, no matter what was going on in my world. And so, I did feel lucky but not for the reason most people would think.

The truth about my mafs experience was simple. It is strange, and surreal, and you have to be a little bit nuts to do it. It pushed me out of my comfort zone in every possible way. It is not real, but not entirely fake. It is scary and exciting all at the same time, and I will always be grateful that I was one of the lucky ones chosen to do it.

I may not have met the love of my life, but I gained something more precious - lifelong friends, a renewed appreciation for my family and home, and a better understanding of how strong I can be. Why 'live the dream' when 'living the reality' is so much better?

CHAPTER 17

IT'S ALL ABOUT TIMING

I have always believed there was one person destined for me and I would know as soon as I met them. Perhaps I was naive. Perhaps the love I had felt was all there was, and that was pretty good. I just didn't understand how people stay together for years without losing interest. The best relationship I had ever seen was that of my son, Daniel and his wife, Jen. They truly love each other. You can tell. They have been together for fifteen years and he still looks at her with absolute adoration. And Jen adores him. They laugh, they are affectionate (but not over the top) and they have no doubt they want to be together.

I have a friend, Rhina, who is the same. She is still besotted with her partner, Patrick, even after 23 years together. They have had their ups and downs and I guess she has dealt with things that would make most people give up. When I ask her "Why do you stay?" she says, "Because he's the one, Missy." Rhina has no doubt and that is the kind of love I always wanted.

I had already been on a few dates with a nice guy before I went on Married at First Sight. We had met on Tinder after one night of me drinking too much and downloading the app. (Sounds like a habit, doesn't it?)

I quickly deleted it the next morning but not before I had received a message from this man, Fred, who said he would like to have a drink together soon.

Timing sure is everything. Sometimes it works well for you. Sometimes against. We would experience both in our brief time together. I felt it was destiny that we even had that conversation. I had only downloaded the app out of boredom (another night with a bottle of wine, the couch and me), and was in the process of trying to delete it the following morning. Fred had just woken up, gone on the app and seen we were a match. His message came through to me seconds before I deleted it.

"Hi there, just saw your message, its lovely to meet you," he wrote.

I looked at his profile again and realised he had been one of the guys I thought looked quite nice. As the "fresh blood" I had received quite a few messages that night, but Fred would be the only one I would actually meet.

"Hi," I wrote. "Nice to talk to you."

We conversed about art, literature and travel and I said I loved the look of his paintings and could I write a story on him for my magazine.

He was keen for a story but more interested in a date, so we decided to meet up at Brass Razu in Mornington when I returned from Darwin the following week.

I was taking my Dad up to see my son and his wife for a family holiday, and we had all been looking forward to it immensely. Lizzy was going as well as Vicky, Steve and little Amy.

Fred and I messaged a couple of times while I was away and decided to meet the Thursday after I returned.

Brass Razu is a lovely little French bar in the Main Street, which I had discovered one day with my Dad. It had become our favourite haunt and they made the best martinis. "Nearly as good as ours love," my father would say.

The décor is just like a little French bistro with provincial lounges, ornate gold trimmed mirrors and framed paintings of Parisian street scenes and the French countryside. There are several little rooms that have intimate areas to sit and enjoy a champagne while getting to know each other, so it is perfect.

I wasn't nervous about the Thursday night date. I had made dating into a social activity rather than trying to meet "the one" and so I was enjoying it so much more. I had a very lovely life and, for the first time, was embracing my single self, without feeling like I was missing something.

I thought Fred sounded very nice, but I also knew that men are great at the start and then things can quickly change so I was living in the moment - a great place to be. I was dating others when I felt like it and I had the Married at First Sight application process still going, so the pressure was off.

It was a rainy and miserable night when I walked into the restaurant. Fred had told me he was waiting in the back room and to meet him there. He had ordered me a glass of French wine and hoped that would be okay. I was immediately impressed that he had taken charge like that (and, let's face it, I love my wine.)

I walked in as confident as ever, wearing my favourite olive green off the shoulder top, white pants and my purple heels.

As soon as I saw him, the air changed. I felt like I had been knocked over and could not believe how handsome he was. He was tall and masculine, and I suddenly felt nervous.

Oh my God. I had no idea this was going to happen. Suddenly, I realised this was not going to be an ordinary date. I didn't know what it was, but this was something I had never felt before.

He stood up to greet me, and I was able to regain my composure. We sat down together on the French lounge and I placed my handbag on the floor beside my feet.

"It is so lovely to finally meet you," he said to me, staring at my eyes, with such self-confidence. "I have been really looking forward to tonight."

"Yes, its lovely to meet you too," I said.

We talked about how funny it was that we nearly missed out on meeting with me trying to delete the app and him just waking up to see our match.

We talked about how much we both love this place, and how much we love Paris and the lifestyle of the French people. I told him about going to France with my father, learning about art and the culture there, and how Paris is now my favourite place in the whole world.

He loved that I was a writer, and I loved that he was an artist. I told him about my family, growing up with an artist uncle who spent his life painting, and that we had his paintings all around our home where I grew up.

I found out that Fred had been married twice before as well, and had several relationships, but broke up with his last wife a couple of years ago. He had just returned from Adelaide where his father lives and had been looking after him for the year before.

We drank wine, laughed and enjoyed a lovely charcuterie, and finished the night with a cognac. Most of the people had left the restaurant, and it was about 11pm and I asked him if he would drive me home. I was still on 000 from my license and would have to leave my car in Mornington.

He drove me home, saw me to the gate and we had a very small kiss, which was lovely.

I went inside thinking what a lovely time I had, and I hoped I would see him again.

The next day, he asked me out and we continued to see each other for the next six weeks.

Then I got the call I was going on MAFS. This is where the bad timing comes in. What to do? I had already signed a contract, and they had put so much time and energy into me, so I felt I had to go through with it. Besides, I had only been seeing the guy for six weeks. For all I knew, he was seeing other people still and, for once in my life, I was going to put myself first and not give up something I wanted for a man. I had spent a lifetime of sacrificing my own needs for the sake of relationships that never worked out anyway. If I was going to learn something from my past mistakes, then I needed to do things differently. "Don't live the same life fifty times" as my Dad would say.

The truth is, deep down, I still didn't trust my judgment. I loved spending time with Fred, that is for sure. We laughed, talked, drank, ate, went to movies, and, when he kissed me, I got butterflies. When I was with him, it felt magic, but I still didn't know what it was.

The night I found out about MAFS, I rang Fred and told him I was going away and we couldn't see each other anymore. I said it was something I had to do, and that I had to be single to do it. That's the crazy thing – I still was single and so was he. You don't usually commit to someone straight away, so I had to get my head clear that this was okay to do.

I spoke to my Dad and Vicky and they said I was giving it way too much thought and it was time for me to have my little adventure.

When I rang Fred that night, it broke my heart, but I had to be strong and put everything into perspective. I hardly knew him. We had been out on a few dates.

"You always do this Melissa, make things out to be bigger than they are," I thought to myself.

It would be several months before Fred and I would see each other again.

I thought of him at times but used every bit of self-discipline I could to just get on with my life, and life was good.

After coming back from doing the show, he was still in my mind, but I wasn't sure if we would ever see each other again.

And then I got the message "Are you back?" on messenger.

We had gone off all social media during the filming of the show so, when he saw me active again, he soon messaged me.

My heart sank. Yes, I was back. Yes, I had been away and married a total stranger and yes, I was now single again. But who would ever be interested in going out with someone with all that new baggage?

Besides that, I couldn't tell him what show I had done. We signed a confidentiality agreement that we didn't talk about it and I took that role very seriously.

He wanted to meet up for a coffee and I agreed but I knew it would probably be the last time I saw him.

CHAPTER 18

THE REAL DEAL

I met Fred at Mr Curtis in Mt Martha in my lunch break a week later. He had finished work early and I had interviews booked for the afternoon, so I had a couple of hours to spare.

The sun was streaming in on the balcony that looks out over the bay and the Mt Martha shops when I saw him sitting there. My heart skipped a beat, and I wondered if it would feel the same way as all those months ago.

The moment I saw him, I knew. He was so handsome sitting there with his white t shirt and blue jeans. He was freshly shaved, and I think he may have just had his hair cut as it looked a bit shorter, but he was exactly the same guy I had met up with all that time ago. And the feeling was magic. Whatever this was, it was still there.

I had filmed a tv show, had lived in an incredible north Sydney apartment, dined at the most beautiful restaurants, and been given the 'star treatment' on Married at First Sight, but this was priceless. This was the feeling I had been missing out on all those years.

I told him about doing the show. I told him John and I were great but no longer together. I told him I was back for good now, and all the time, I wondered what his situation was.

It was like starting all over again. He had been free to do as he wanted for months. Was he seeing anyone? Did he feel the same?

Would he be able to handle the MAFS news that I had just laid out on the table?

And that's when I knew, sitting on the balcony of Mr Curtis, looking out over the water. This was the man for me. He didn't care that I had gone of a tv show. He didn't care that I had married a total stranger on national television. He just wanted me; however he could get me.

I had never experienced anything like this. Was it possible that this, right here, was the love of my life?

It certainly was the most tumultuous start to a relationship that I had ever had but it just felt right. And so, we picked up where we had left off. We went out to the movies, he cooked for me, we spent whole weekends at his apartment near the water, we listened to French radio, and we fell in love.

I told my Dad I was seeing someone who was an artist and he didn't ask many questions. I think he knew that I would tell him if it got serious and Dad was very good at giving me my privacy and space. I think he trusted that I would find my own way now and wasn't the confused and unconfident woman I used to be. I had finally learnt to trust my own judgement and my Dad could tell.

Very soon, Fred asked me to go on a holiday with him to Paris.

"Paris?' I thought. "Sure, I would love to, but how on earth can I do that?"

The show was well and truly over, and they were starting to promote the next season so I was no longer in the spotlight, but I still felt like I didn't know if I should.

Again, I spoke to my Dad, knowing he would say "you don't miss out on going to Paris love." Which of course he did. So, before I knew it, we were on a flight to France. Now this would be the real test for us. We had never spent more than two full days together and this was for over two weeks. I hoped we would get on well because, deep down, I wanted this to be my forever thing, but I had been burnt so many times.

Fred had organised all the tickets and accommodation and all I had to do was show up.

I organised for Lizzy to stay with friends who would look after her at our home and met Fred at his apartment for our drive up to the airport.

Time went by differently when I was with him, and our 23-hour flight felt went by so quickly. We held hands, watched movies, drank champagne, and laughed like two excited kids.

We stayed in Montmartre which was my favourite place in Paris. I had discovered it ten years before when I went to France with my Dad. We had wandered around the streets there, drank wine on outdoor tables and even found a wonderful double bass player performing Simon and Garfunkel's 'Sound of Silence' which was something my father ended up devoting a poem to years later.

Fred loved Montmartre the moment we got there. We went in the tiny little elevator to our upstairs room, with French windows opening to the courtyard, a double bed and inset wardrobe either side.

We quickly got changed and went for a stroll along the cobble stone streets, down the alley ways, and found a charming little café where we sat outside and enjoyed a glass of bubbles, toasting to our new adventure.

It was easy to be in the moment with Fred. For the first time, I knew what it was like to be with someone who was feeling the same as me. My father had always taught me the importance of being yourself when you travel, taking in the culture and being respectful to the people who live there. Fred was all of these. The way he spoke to the waiters and shopkeepers was beautiful and he tried to use his limited French which I found delightful.

The next two weeks were heaven as we fell more and more in love with each moment. We visited galleries, drank cocktails, and became familiar with our little area, walking around the streets every day, wandering into cafes and starting to become better at speaking French.

Now I knew what love was. I knew because I was just as happy being with Fred in Rosebud as I was in the streets of Paris. I knew because the magic feeling never left and every time I looked at him, I thought he was so handsome. He was smart, kind, creative and I had finally met the man I wanted to be with.

When I came home, I had to tell my father. I knew that he would be so excited for me but didn't want to worry him that I was going to lose my head over this relationship.

"Dad, guess what?" I said to him, one day when I had gone over to his house for lunch, on my return.

Dad was starting to wilt a bit. I could see that he was losing his zest for life a little and spending more and more time in front of the television. He was now 88 and tired, so our lunches had become less venturing out to restaurants and more me bringing a pie over from the bakery.

"What?" he turned to me and asked.

"I had the best time in Paris, Dad. Fred is the nicest guy and we got on so well," I said excitedly. "I don't want to worry you but I'm pretty sure he is the one."

Dad looked at me intensely, like he was thinking of exactly the right words to say. I suddenly felt scared. What if he didn't like him. What if he didn't approve. It was so important to me to have Dad's support. He always knew what was best for me, usually before I did.

He suddenly got a twinkle in his eye, and a smirk started to appear on his face.

"Yes love. I know," he said. "He's the real deal."

As usual, my father knew before me. He knew that I was falling in love. He knew that Paris would seal the deal, and he, too, knew that this was 'my love'.

I looked at my Dad and wondered if I would ever be as wise as him and hoped that, one day, I could give my own children the same quiet confidence that he gave me. I thought how lucky I was to now have two great men in my life, and everything that happened before was leading up to this point.

CHAPTER 19

A LINK OF GOSSAMER THREAD

I have learnt to be a strong woman. I have survived marriage breakups, loved ones in car accidents, and health scares when I didn't know if I would live to see my children grow up. I have lost jobs and gained new ones, moved homes, and watched my adult children relocate to other states and countries. I have witnessed grandchildren born and my parents get older.

All in all, I have not let many things unsettle me. That all changed when my father became terminally ill.

Dad and I had been going to the doctor almost every week and he was becoming more concerned with his medical appointments than our social engagements. His shaking hands were struggling to put the kettle on when I went over for a weekly coffee with a custard tart from the local bakery, and his daily walks had become less frequent as he complained of being "too tired".

Even our Sunday mass and lunches were becoming further apart. I would ring Dad the night before and say, "We still on for Mass tomorrow?" and most of the time he would say "Not this week love. I think I might just have a quiet one."

I knew there was something wrong but didn't want to believe it. Not my Dad. This happens to everyone, I know, but not him.

Dad and I eventually moved into a little house together in Safety Beach to assist me with paying rent and so Dad could have someone close by to help him out. I was in dire straits financially, and Dad was struggling physically so it seemed the perfect idea. Coming back from doing the show and not working for three months had created a huge pile of bills that was hard to manage. You do get paid what they call "out of pocket expenses" (they can't call it a wage as we are not actors), but it is minimal and, as usual, Dad was my saviour.

The master bedroom and little lounge room where he spent the majority of his time were becoming depressing. Every morning, without fail I would hear the clunk, clunk, clunk of his cane walking down the tiled hallway from his room to the kitchen, the kettle goes on, cup rattles and the teaspoon is plopped on the saucer. Then shuffle, shuffle and plonk, the coffee is placed on the side table before Dad would settle himself in the recliner which made a noise like a 'sigh' every time he sat down.

He would reach for the remote control, and within seconds the noise of morning television would be on, usually overly excited hosts on the Today Show on Channel Nine.

It was his ritual, but I knew he wasn't happy. Dad had been so active all his life. If he wasn't physically well, then he made sure he mentally kept alert with quizzes and his love of literature and poetry.

Dad had only recently applied again for Millionaire Hot Seat and had won Sale of the Century ten years before.

His spark was fading. My Dad was disappearing in front of my eyes. And he was becoming skinnier. His clothes started to hang off him and he either didn't care, or he didn't notice. He was no longer 'raging against the dying of the light'. He was giving in to it, I could tell.

The day the doctor told Dad his cancer had spread is still burned into my mind.

After having an aortic aneurism, a year before, regular check-ups were part of the deal and this time we had to take Dad for an ultrasound to make sure the suture was still in place and healed.

My sister had come down to take Dad to his appointment, and it was not what they had expected to see.

When Dad got home, he said the ultrasound technician had looked concerned and called another specialist in to consult. They didn't tell Dad what it was but said we had to go to his lovely Dr Sweety for the results.

Dad knew it was bad. We all did. He had lost his appetite and so much weight and he looked grey. I had only ever seen that colour once in my life, many years before, and it is something you never forget.

An old journo I used to work with, Mike Morris, had cancer but still insisted on coming to the office. His writing was everything to him. I saw him at the bottom of the stairs one morning. His face was grey, and he was struggling to take a breath but insisted on walking up the stairs by himself.

"You go up first, Melissa," he said to me this morning. "I'll be right behind you. I just need to take my time."

I walked up the stairs and waited for Mike to follow me. When he eventually got in the door, he collapsed and died in front of my eyes. I have never forgotten Mike, what a wonderful man he was, and I felt honoured to be the last person he spoke to. But I have also never forgotten that look - that grey, lifeless look.

I thought Dr Sweety was going to cry when he told Dad the news.

As usual when Dad and I got into the doctor's rooms, Dad would hand me his walking stick and white 'Bloody Long Walk' cap that my daughter, Antoinette had given him after completing the 30km walk, and he wore it so proudly. It was as if he had done the walk with her.

Dr Sweety looked more serious today as he turned to his computer to go through the test results with Dad. He looked at the screen intently, as if he was making sure they were still the same, that by some miracle they hadn't changed overnight.

He leaned forward. "David," he said with a worried look. "As you know we found some markers on your ultrasound that we didn't expect. They are showing secondary cancers in the liver, bowel, and partly in your spine. I am so sorry, but it looks like you are in the fourth stage of cancer."

Dad sat back on his chair, as if the information had knocked the wind out of him.

After a few seconds, he said "Okay Doc, what do we do?"

Dad always had a plan when faced with challenges. He would say to me "Define the problem, and then you can find a solution."

This time he didn't.

Dad thought very highly of Dr Sweety and trusted his judgement and advice. He leaned forward and was hanging off his every word.

The doctor said that he was so very sorry but there was nothing that could be done now. Dad's ultrasound, along with the blood test results indicated the cancer had spread to the point of being irreversible. It was now a matter of making him comfortable and ensuring quality of life. He talked about pain management and the options Dad had with medicinal marijuana, and strong analgesics. We would be given a referral to Peter Mac for a specialist opinion, but Dr Sweety thought the prognosis did not look good.

We drove home in silence. There was nothing left to say.

For the next six months, a nurse called in on a regular basis to see Dad, help him with his catheter which had become a regular fixture, talk about pain levels, and weigh him.

And I did not cope. I was living in the same house as my father but there was a great divide between us. He was trying to process what was happening to him. He was scared and angry and I felt the same. I pushed him away. He was the man who had been my entire world, the person who I loved with all my heart, but why could I not show it?

I didn't understand. I knew that one day I would not hear that clunk clunk clunk of the walking stick coming down the hallway. I knew that one day he wouldn't be sitting in that chair with his cup of coffee and morning television. And I knew that one day he would not be there when I got home from work, saying "Hi Missy, is that you? How was your day, love?" Yet I still couldn't bring myself to let my guard down. That awkward feeling between Dad and I was back, and I was paralysed. The only thing I knew for sure was this would be my biggest regret - that I couldn't tell my father how I felt.

Sometimes we would sit outside and have a glass of wine and a cigarette and talk about the world and our days, but those moments had become rare. He loved our chats but got tired very easily, and I found it hard to look at him. I didn't want him to see me with pity in my eyes, but most importantly, I didn't want him to see my fear.

Every now and again, we would have a magic moment, listening to some music, or watching an old movie Dad loved, or him reading me his latest poem he was working on but the only time I saw him truly joyous was when he had visits from his great granddaughters, Amy and Stephanie. It was then, with their innocent smiles and carefree giggles that my Dad felt alive again, and I witnessed the unspoken connection between those at the start of their lives, and those at the end – a link of gossamer thread.

CHAPTER 20

EVERYBODY DESERVES A DISASTER

My Dad died on May 3, 2019, in a palliative care hospital in Frankston. His body was riddled with cancer, but his heart and soul were intact. He had started writing a poem in his final year of living. He was fed up with being sick, fed up with feeling sorry for himself and I guess tired of life and trying to make sense of it the only way he knew how - with words. His hands were shaky from the cancer drugs but also from the stroke he had suffered ten years before, but he insisted on writing in a notebook he kept beside his bed.

Dad would sit in his chair beside the bed, writing on the over bed table. On cool days, the sun streamed in through the windows that framed a courtyard filled with agapanthus and bright pink azaleas. He always loved his gardens and made every place he lived look beautiful. Dad had been in the palliative care ward for seven weeks so far and spent hours looking out at those flowers. When we sat outside, he would look to the sky and say, "the world is beautiful, life is sweet."

When I asked him what his latest poem was called, he said "Everybody deserves a Disaster" love and proceeded to explain to me what that meant.

When Dad wanted to explain something important, he would have a long think for a while, his hand furrowing his brow to make sure the words came out just right. I knew when he did this, the answer was bound to be a good one. He looked up from his notebook, placed his pen neatly on the table and looked me in the eye.

"I have been struggling with my own personal demons, love. I have never felt as sorry for myself as I have in this past year. I have been angry at my situation, pissed off with the world and found very little joy. I sit at home all day and don't have the strength or energy to go out. I have a bag of piss tied to my leg, and I cannot even stand up long enough to go for a walk without falling down. My body is slowly giving up on me and I feel like I'm dying. But I have always been philosophical, and these are the things that I know for sure, and I want you to know them too."

His voice broke as if he was about to break down in tears and I knew in that moment this would be something I would never forget. He said:

"Life is beautiful and difficult and challenging. We all face disasters in our life. For some it is health problems, for others it might be money or personal relationships. Some have disaster thrust upon them and hitting them from left field and others bring it upon themselves. The important thing to remember is our disasters are what make us who we are. They are our chance to stretch our limits and reinvent our self-belief. It is only by the bad things that happen that we truly know how strong we can be.

I have seen that throughout life. I saw it from a young child, growing up in the depression. We had no money and little food and we survived by our strength and character. My mother taught me the power of positive thinking and it is my wish that I pass this on to you.

In my 89 years, I have seen all sides of the human spirit from the most callous and cruel acts of evil to miracles and human kindness in its purest form. I have witnessed wars where good men have to kill each other to survive. I have lived through the depression when we had nothing. I have learnt that we live alone, and we die alone, and what happens in between is totally in our control. I have learnt that life can surprise us, and we have the capability to do great things with small deeds. I have learnt that there is nothing better than the feeling of a small child's arms wrapped around your neck and nothing that makes you happier than the sound of children laughing. I have dined with Kissinger, flown the concord on its last flight, and shared a meal in a Bedouin tent. I have travelled to all sorts of places, met the most incredible people and experienced the joy of coming home. I have spent a lifetime searching for adventure and only realised that everything I needed was right in front of me with you and your sisters.

I have learnt that our greatest strength begins with our minds and I have seen people will themselves to live and to die. I thought I could overcome everything, but I now understand that I cannot overcome this, and I need to make the most of the time I have left."

As I sat on Dad's walker facing him, his shaking frail hands reached out to me and he said, with tears streaming down his face "My greatest fear for you my daughter is that you will never know how good you are."

I knew he was right. Dad is always right. He was talking about self-belief, and I knew that what he told me was the reason for my book. I finally knew what I had been writing all these years that our disasters are an opportunity to learn and grow and, once again, my Dad had guided me on the right path.

I miss my father more than words can describe. I have his tweed hat and walking stick hanging in my room. His chess table and chair are still set up where he left it as if he is going to show up and play. The carved wooden statue he made from a tree that fell down on his Woodend property takes pride of place in the lounge room and I think about him all the time.

When my father died, my sister and I were sitting either side of his bed. He had taken a bad turn the night before and never recovered. I wasn't there for him that night and it is something I have had to forgive myself for. By the time I got there, he never woke up.

I was there when he took his final breath. We were playing Don McLean on the iPad, drinking red wine, and reminiscing about the wonderful nights around his dining room table, listening to our favourite singers and solving the problems of the world, and my father drifted away.

I don't know where he is now, but I feel him around me all the time and whenever I have a problem I say, "What would Dad do?"

My father had five rules to live by which he called Carr's Law. They grace his tomb stone today:

Survive.

Pain is inevitable, misery is a choice.

Treasure quiet moments.

Never look for gratitude, just do it.

When disaster looms, all you have left is style.

ABOUT THE AUTHOR

Melissa Walsh has been working as a published author for 25 years in print media, while completing two degrees at university as a mature aged student. She began her career in freelance journalism at the age of 30, writing the real estate guide for local newspapers as well as magazine and feature articles. Melissa has written a monthly magazine for the Mornington Peninsula, focusing on lifestyle, celebrity and inspirational stories, and now runs her own business, Melissa Marie Media and Events.

A mother of four, and grandmother of two, Melissa is committed to breaking stereotypes, which was shown by her appearance on Channel Nine's Married at First Sight, the first grandmother to be cast on the reality show. She wrote her first novella at the age of 21 about her experience of being a teenage mother and continues to write about her treacherous relationship history in her new bio-novel, *Everybody Deserves a Disaster.*

Connect with Melissa

Instagram: @melissa_mafs
LinkedIn: **linkedin.com/in/melissa-walsh-0a056919**
Web Site: **mmmediaandevents.com.au**

Printed in Great Britain
by Amazon

47250564R00068